The Mystical Tales Of Indus Valley

Wizards Of Hastin

by P. Ashar

www.MysticalValley.com

First Edition

Any resemblance to actual events or persons, living or dead, is entirely coincidental.

"The Mystical Tales of Indus Valley: Wizards of Hastin," by P. Ashar. ISBN 1-58939-838-6.

Manufactured in the United States of America.

Dedicated To:

All Humanity

"Give peace a chance,"

as John Lennon once said.

Thanks to Jeff Crosby and Thomas McAteer for beautifully illustrating the book.

My special thanks to the co-writer of the book, my former teacher Thomas.J.P.

I want to thank Opal Infotech, India for beautifully creating www.<u>Mystical Valley</u>.com for me.

For my parents,

my wife,

and my sisters,

who always make me feel loved every single day.

This book is adapted from the great epic "The Mahabharata"

The approximate occurrence date of this event is around 2000 BC. The book is recreated with western audiences in mind. The great epic has been confined to only the eastern cultures of the world. It has hardly reached the western world.

The recreated book has characters from Roman and Greek mythology to appeal to western audiences.

The book will interest children, young adults, adults and elderly alike.

P. Ashar

$\mathscr{I}$NTRODUCTION

This is an epic tale about two mighty families who are cousins. They are descendants of King Sudry of Hastin, who belonged to the Lunar dynasty.

The tale describes the power struggle and jealousy between the two families. One family is called the Telhoths and the other is called the Prols. They both want to rule the Kingdom of Hastin.

It concludes with a great war in which the main characters use mystical supernatural powers, plots, politics, cunningness, bravery and wisdom against each other.

The forces of evil represent the Telhoths and the forces of good represent the Prols.

There are five Prol brothers and one hundred wicked Telhoth brothers and one sister.

The five Prol brothers are Vilmaril (the eldest, wise and generous), Hugo (the second eldest of the Prol brothers, also *the biggest and bravest), Trilock (the world's best archer), and Nakula and Shakula (the twins).*

The two main Telhoth characters are Assura, the eldest and the cruelest of the Telhoth brothers, who wants the Kingdom of Hastin for himself, and Amon, who is the second eldest of the Telhoth brothers and a blind follower of his elder brother the cruel Assura.

The Prols rule the kingdom at first, but lose the throne to the Telhoths when the wicked eldest brother Assura cheats Vilmaril at a game of dice. The Prols are exiled to the forest for thirteen years. The last year they are exiled in disguise. The Telhoths refuse to hand back the throne to the Prols after the agreed period of exile. Because they are brave warriors, the Prols know that they have no choice but to declare war on their cheating cousins. With Mohan, the god on their side and because of the strength of their supernatural powers, the Prols declare the war on the Telhoths, called the battle of Goibur.

Events that lead to the great war are full of mystery, greed, wisdom, politics, cunningness, lies, truth and compassion, which should guide us to live our life ethically, peacefully, and with moral values.

Welcome to the world of mysticism and adventure.

P.Ashar

LUNAR DYNASTY FAMILY CHART

THE PROLS	THE TELHOTHS
PROL: Younger brother of Lohas; King; retired from kingdom to hunt and enjoy life.Has two wives Noralius and Madri.	LOHAS: Blind elder brother of Prol; becomes patriarch, king; takes charge of Kingdom after Prol's retirement. Has a wife named Wardoria.
NORALIUS: Wife of Prol; has three sons, Vilmaril, Hugo, and Trilock. MADRI: Second wife of Prol, mother of Nakula and Shakula.	WARDORIA: Blindfolded wife of Lohas, jealous of Noralius who had a son first; queen mother of a hundred cruel sons.

THE WARRING COUSINS

VILMARIL: First son of Noralius. Wise and generous. Always truthful. He has a weakness for dice gambling. HUGO: Second son of Noralius, son of the wind god; strong as thunder. With Deolana, goddess of the forest sires Fioril, who later assists him in war. TRILOCK: Third son of Noralius and perfect warrior and world's best archer, born to conquer. SHAKULA and NAKULA: Twin sons of Madri, representing patience and wisdom.They are step brothers of Vilmaril, Hugo and Trilock. All five Prol brothers love each other dearly.	KARNA: First son of Noralius, sired by the Sun god; left to drift in a basket. Brought up by chariot driver. Unrecognized by his mother, Karna fights for the Telhoths. ASSURA: First son of Wardoria; fierce angry leader of Telhoths, "comes to destroy." AMON: Son of Wardoria; drags Arywiel by hair. He is the younger brother of cruel, Assura.

OTHERS RELATIVES, COUNSELORS, ALLIES

ARYWIEL: Daughter of king Aruvious; won by Trilock in a contest; wife of the five Prols

MOHAN: Cousin of Noralius, Mohan serves as spiritual and military counselor and friend to the whole family--both Prols and Telhoths.

LIRAN: Teenage son of Trilock. Volunteers to go to the battlefield. Heroic and brave. Gets trapped in the "Web of Snakes."

SAKUNI: Uncle of Assura, younger brother of Wardoria. An expert dice player; suggests and plays the dice game with the Prols to trap them.

GODASH: Uncle and noble counselor to King Lohas; raises both Prols and Tclhoths, but leads in battle for the Telhoths. The gods have given him the power to choose the time of his death.

DRONA: Teacher of cousins. Cares for Prols & and Telhoths; mighty warrior himself.

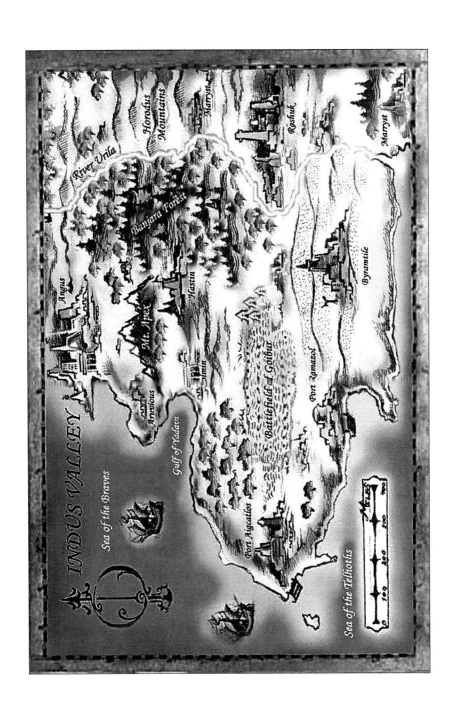

TABLE OF CONTENTS

BACKGROUND:

BLUNDERS OF
KING SUDRY:

King Sudry was a powerful king who belonged to the Lunar dynasty. He ruled the mighty Kingdom Of Hastin.

He was a great lover of hunting. Once while he was out hunting in the forest, he came to a river where he saw a beautiful lady bathing in the river water. The king was enchanted by the beauty of the lady and offered to marry her. The lady agreed to marry him on one condition. After marriage, the king should never question any of her actions. Without knowing the implications of this one condition, the king agreed because he was so deeply in love with her. Soon they were married and lived happily for some time. When their first child was born, the lady took the child secretly to the river and threw the child in the gushing waters of the river Urila to be drowned. The king quickly learned of this but he was bound by his promise not to question his wife and kept quiet. When the second child was born, the lady did the same thing, and again the king was helpless. This continued until their seventh child was born.

The king was puzzled and inconsolable but he could not do anything for fear of his losing his wife's love. When their eighth child was born, the king could no longer control himself, and he asked his wife, "My dear lady, why do you kill our children in this cruel manner?" The wife was infuriated and said; "Now you have broken your promise and I can't stay here any more". But before she left she told the king the reason of her strange behavior. Actually, she was Urila, the river goddess. While she was in heaven, the eight Arol brothers who were gods had everything they could desire to make them happy. But they were not happy. In their hearts they constantly craved for things. Then one day their greedy eyes fell on a deer that belonged to a sage. The deer was so beautiful that they wanted her instantly. They planned and plotted together trying to find ways to get the deer. Eventually they decided to steal her. However, when the moment came to do so, the seven older brothers panicked and decided not to take that kind of action for fear of the sage. The youngest Arol brother was ready to do the deed. He stole the deer and brought the deer to his brothers and together they hid her away. The sage came to know about this and was filled with grief. He cursed all of them in anger for their sin. The brothers would fall from their high estate, he said, and be born on the earth as mortal men, for they did not deserve to be gods. Heaven and its joys were not meant for sinful creatures such as them!

The words of the sage struck fear and sorrow in to the hearts of Arol brothers. They did not wish to be born as mortals. Mortals must suffer pain and sorrow and have to eventually die. They immediately begged the sage to forgive them. The sage's heart melted and he relented. He said he cannot take away the curse but he could soften the curse and make it easier for them to bear.

He told them that for seven older brothers who had only sinned in thought, desiring the deer and plotting how to get her, their life on earth will be short, the space of only few hours. However the youngest brother who had done the deed must suffer. He must spend a full lifetime on the earth as a mortal. But he would be a mortal above all other mortals and would live a life of such wisdom and glory that his name would be known all over the earth and in heaven, and all men would honor him!

"Leave now." Sage continued in a kinder tone. "Go to the river Goddess Urila and she will help you."

The Arols did what they were told. They pleaded to her and told her their sad story. She decided out of pity that she will come down to the earth and will give birth to the eight Arol brothers. As soon as they are born, in that same hour, she will take away the child and put an end to their lives so that their life on the earth may soon be ended and they may return to their heavenly home. She agreed to do this and so she helped the first seven Arols to be emancipated from the earthly existence. Now only the last child was left. "I will take him along with me to heaven to learn all kinds of mystic arts and bring him back to earth when he reaches adulthood". So saying, the Goddess Urila disappeared and left for her heavenly abode.

The king was greatly distressed at the sudden disappearance of his wife, decided to give up his life of pleasure, and became almost an ascetic, leading a life of penance and self-restraint.

Years latter the king was roaming around on the banks of the river when he chanced to a see a young lad of very pleasing appearance. The lad seemed to be well versed in the art of archery. The king saw that the lad was shooting arrows in the gushing waters of the river and was building up a bridge with the help of the arrows in order to stop the swirling waters of the river from flooding. Just then, there appeared before him a beautiful lady of bewitching beauty. But King Sudry could not recognize her. She revealed to him that she was Urila, his wife, and the young lad was no other than their eighth child, whose name was Godash. "This is our child whom I have brought up and taught him all the arts and science of warfare and all the knowledge of philosophy from the gods. Please take him with you." So saying the lady disappeared. King Sudry took the lad with him and went back to his kingdom.

KING SUDRY MARRIES AGAIN

King Sudry was very happy with Godash and soon declared him crown prince. Godash grew in wisdom, knowledge and piety. Four years passed in this way when a strange event took place which changed everything. While the king was wandering on the banks of the river, he smelt a powerful fragrance coming from somewhere. He followed the scent, which led him to a lovely lady who lived near the river. She happened to be the daughter of a fisherman. Her name was Yavati. No sooner did the king see her than he fell in love with her. He forgot all his asceticism and asked the lady to marry him. The lady would not submit till her father had given his consent. The father was very happy to have a king as his son-in-law, but he put this condition to the king, "You must promise that the child born of my daughter will be the king after you." Though the king was enchanted by the beauty of the maid, he could not bind himself to this condition as Godash was his first son and heir apparent. Though love-lorn, the king returned to Hastin without Yavati. The king could not, however, concentrate on anything else and his health began to deteriorate. He took no interest in food, drink or sport. Godash, who was intelligent, did not fail to see the sudden change in his father's health. He was worried but could not understand the reason for his father's failing health. After a few days, he made himself bold enough to ask his father, "My dear father, since your return from the forest you have not been at all at ease and your health is declining daily. Please tell me the reason for this." The king said that he was worried because he had only one son. He wondered how his progeny would be carried on if something happened to his only son. This answer did not satisfy Godash.

Godash summoned the charioteer who had lead the father to the river and asked him what had happened on their trip there. Hesitatingly the charioteer revealed how the king had fallen in love with Yavati, the daughter of the fisherman, but could not marry her because of the strange demand of her father. Now Godash understood the real reason for the failing health of his father. Straight away, he took the same charioteer and went to the hut of the fisherman on the bank of the river. The prince said, "I have come to take my stepmother to the kingdom of Hastin." But, the fisherman said, "I am highly honored by the visit of the royal guest but what about my condition? You are the heir apparent to the throne. How will my grandson ascend the throne as long as you are there?" Godash at once pronounced, "I disown all my right to be the king after my father's death. Your grandson will become the king. I will never claim the title of king. You can thus rest assured. I hereby solemnly renounce all my right to be the future king. Are you now satisfied?" The fisherman was very happy but he wanted to make doubly sure that Godash's sons and grandsons would not claim the right to the throne. So he asked him again, "What guarantee do I have that your sons and grandsons would not demand the throne in future?" Godash then solemnly declared that he would remain a celibate all his life and would never get married so there would not be any question of his progeny ascending the throne of Hastin. The gods in heaven were overjoyed by this solemn promise of Godash and showered him with flower petals from heaven, shouting loudly, "Godash, Godash" which means a person who takes a solemn vow and fulfills it.

With the consent of the fisherman-chieftain, Godash escorted his new stepmother mother Yavati to the palace and produced her before his father. The father could not believe his eyes. He was so proud of his son that he showered on him the boon 'DEATH AT WILL.' In other words, death would not touch him until he wished to die. Later, King Sudry came to know that Yavati was not the daughter of the fisherman but of a king. She was simply brought up by the fisherman chief since the age of twelve. He therefore married her according to the sacred rituals and later she gave birth to two sons, Zolos and Virzos.

After the death of King Sudry, Godash became the guardian of the two boys. Zolos became the king soon, but he died an early death. Virzos then was crowned king. Godash continued to guide the young ruler.

⚙HE ⚙HREE 🏰RINCESSE':

𝕵 n the olden days, royal marriages were of two types: Marriage by choice and an extraordinary marriage in which the suitor snatched away the bride by force. The king of Romazol had three daughters: Amba, Ambika and Ambalika. The usual marriage by choice was arranged by the king for his daughters in which Godash took part. All were shocked to see this man. Everybody knew Godash's vow of celibacy and his vow of never getting married. Nevertheless, Godash declared that he would carry away all the three maidens by force to be brides for Virzos. No one was able to challenge him. Thus, he brought the three maidens to Hastin.

At Hastin, Amba, the eldest, pleaded with Godash that she had already chosen Salva, the king of Saubala, as her husband, so she was taken there. Virzos married the other two sisters, but before they could give him a son, he died. Mother Yavati entreated with Godash to get married to the two widows and thus give a suitable successor to the throne of Hastin but Godash reminded her of his solemn vow of celibacy. They thought of a possible solution. The widows could unite with a holy man, a sage of the highest order. Only the sage Yasa fulfilled such a criterion.

THE BLIND, THE PALE AND THE POOR:

In this context Yavati narrated her own experience of the past. As a young maid she was escorting the great sage, Parasara, in a boat across the Urila. On the way the sage united with her and as a result a dark child was born to her. The child became a great wise sage called sage Yasa, and thus sage Yasa was the elder half-brother of Zolos and Virzos. Sage Yasa was called upon by Yavati and was requested to give children to Ambika and Ambalika.

The two daughters were asked to wait for the arrival of the sage at their bedchambers. When Ambika saw the dark colored and ugly looking sage, she was so frightened that she closed her eyes. As a result, she gave birth to a blind child who was called Lohas and who later became the king in the Telhoth line.

When Ambalika saw the ugly figure of the sage, she turned pale and as a result gave birth to Prol, the pale in color. Yavati also requested the sage to give one more child to Ambika as the first one was blind. However, Ambika sent her maid in her place and so she begot a son whom she named Vidura who was not of royal line. Godash continued to be the protector, preceptor and guide to all the young princes who were educated in all the different skills and learnings.

After consulting Vidura, Godash arranged to find a suitable match for Lohas in the family of Aruvious. King Zarus was at first unwilling to give his daughter to a blind man but after considering his royal lineage, he agreed to give his daughter, Wardoria, in marriage. Upon finding out that her husband-to-be was blind, Wardoria swore never to enjoy what he could not and blindfolded herself. For the rest of her life, she wore the blindfold covering her eyes and thus respect her husband.

$\mathcal{B}$IRTH $\mathcal{OF}$ $\mathcal{P}$ROL $\mathcal{A}$ND $\mathcal{C}$ELHOTH $\mathcal{B}$ROTHERS:

Noralius, princess of Romak had served the great sage, Zykos, as a young girl. Sage Zykos was so pleased by her care and service that he taught her a mantra, a sacred formula to invoke and call upon any god whenever she wished. Without realizing the mantra's significance, Noralius one day uttered the formula for fun and called upon the Sun-God. At once, the Sun-God appeared before her and demanded to unite with her in marriage. Soon she begot a son whom she cast away in the river by placing him in a basket. This baby later became the famous warrior named Karna who will fight for the evil Telhoth brothers.

As Lohas was blind, Godash crowned Prol the king. He also got him married to Noralius. After some time Prol got another queen, Madri. Later on Prol performed several heroic acts, which pleased Godash very much. Prol was very fond of hunting and always took both his wives on hunting expeditions. Once he shot an arrow at a mating pair of deer, which brought upon him the curse that if ever he embraced his wife in passion, it would bring about his death. Thus, he remained childless and almost became an ascetic, but he worried about his progeny. Then Noralius told him about the secret mantra given to her by sage Zykos. He told her to invoke the God of Righteousness. In this manner, they got their first child whom they named Vilmaril, the resolute in war. Then Noralius invoked the wind god and begot Hugo. Later the king of the gods gave her Trilock. After this, Noralius taught the mantra to Madri, Prol's second queen, who chanted the mantra and invited the Lord of thunder who gave her the twin sons, Nakula and Shakula. These were the five Prol brothers.

Wardoria, the wife of Lohas, also became pregnant but could not give birth for a long time. Being angered by this, she gave a severe blow to her belly, which aborted into lump of flesh. Just then Sage Yasa came there, divided the lump into pieces, and put them into a pot. From there came out a hundred sons and a daughter; the eldest was named Assura who would ultimately be the cause of the destruction of the Telhoth family. All these hundred sons were called the Telhoths.

While the five Prol brothers were undergoing their education, Prol one day embraced his wife Madri with passion and so died on the spot. The Prols came back to

Godash. But there was bad news waiting. Sage Yasa appeared secretly to Yavati and told her that bad days were awaiting the Telhoth family. Thus Yavati decided to go to the forest along with Ambika and Ambalika and spend the remaining days in peace and penance.

EXPLOITS OF HUGO:

Now Godash had the heavy duty of looking after all the grandsons, the Prols and the Telhoths. There was intense rivalry among the brothers and cousins. Hugo with his antics always outsmarted the Telhoths, especially the ambitious Assura who wanted to occupy the coveted place of Vilmaril. Once Assura arranged a picnic on a riverbank where he plotted to kill Hugo by giving him food mixed with poison. With the effect of the poison, Hugo went into a deep sleep and the Telhoth brothers tied him and threw him into the river.

Soon the Prols came to know that Hugo was missing and they went back and searched the whole river-surroundings thoroughly but to no avail. Then Noralius, who suspected some foul play, sent for Vidura. Vidura assured Noralius not to worry as the Prols were going to lead a long life as was foretold by the great sage.

In the meantime, Hugo, who was lying in the deep waters of the river under the influence of the poison, was soon surrounded by poisonous snakes that started biting him on all sides. This snake poison acted as an antidote to the other poison, which Assura had given him. The snakes reported this whole episode to Vasuki, the king of the snake-land. Vasuki recognized Hugo, the son of Noralius, fed him with the nectar of strength, and sent him back to his mother. Assura was again disappointed.

When King Sudry was still alive, he found a boy and a girl in the forest while he was hunting. He brought them home and carefully looked after them. He named them Kripa and Kripi. This Kripa later became proficient in archery and he was put in charge of teaching archery to all the princes. Thus began the great school of archery where princes from other land also came to learn.

Once a strange incident took place in this school of archery. A ball fell into a nearby well while the princes were playing a game. No one knew how to retrieve the ball from the bottom of the well. Just then, a stranger happened to arrive. He told the princes that the ball could be removed from the well by the skill of archery. The princes wondered how that could be done. The stranger threw his ring into the well. Then he took a few blades of grass and, weaving them into arrows, he shot them one after another into the well, the first striking and sticking to the ball and the others hanging on to one another. Thus he could easily remove the ball by the string of grass

When grandfather heard of this event, he immediately understood that this stranger could only be Drona, the renowned archery teacher. He was at once summoned and asked to be the teacher of the princes. Drona agreed to this.

THE TEACHER AND HIS POOR DISCIPLE:

Drona was the son of a famous sage. After his studies, he took up the study of archery and became highly proficient in that art. During that time, he also became a close friend of another student, Anga, the prince of Angus who promised Drona that he would never forget him and would share his wealth when he became the king of Angus.

Time passed and in due course Drona married Kripi and they had a son whom they named Ashwa. In order to learn all the secrets of archery, Drona approached Sage Lukotos and under his guidance became an ace archer. In spite of all this knowledge, Drona was a poor man and could not afford even to give milk to his son. It was then that he remembered his good old school mate, Anga, who had now become the king of Angus and decided to approach him for help.

He went up to him in his palace and said, "Dear friend, do you remember me? I am Drona, your companion in the school. Do you still remember the promise you made to me during our stay in the school?" However, Anga was a changed man now. He did not want to remember his childhood friend and and his silly dreams. He spurned Drona saying, "Childhood fancies are not realities and a pauper can not become the friend of a prince." This insulted Drona and he left the palace there and then, making up his mind to teach a good lesson to his friend some time in life.

Drona was now in Hastin where his brother-in-law, Kripa, lived and where Godash appointed him the teacher of the Prol and Telhoth princes. Princes from other kingdoms also joined this school of archery. Among all these students, Trilock was unique, not only in his mastery over weapons and archery but also in his devotion to duty and his master.

Once Gorodus, a youthful hunter, happened to come to that academy and pleaded with the master to accept him as a student. However, Drona refused to admit him as a pupil since he was a mere hunter. Disappointed, Gorodus went back to the forest, made a clay image of Drona, and paying his respects to him began to practice archery. Gorodus was never admitted to the archery school but he managed to learn the skill through his great dedication and his ability to visualize that Drona was actually teaching him personally every day, every moment. Because of his extraordinary devotion, he was able to acquire the highest proficiency in archery.

One day the princes of the Telhoth house went on a hunting expedition into the forest. Their dog, who accompanied them, wandered astray and was seen by Gorodus. The dog began to bark at the ugly looking lad. Gorodus shot a number of arrows to stop the dog from barking without causing him any harm. When the Telhoth brothers saw this, they were wonderstruck. They asked the lad who he was and the boy gave his name as Gorodus. He further said that he was a disciple of Drona, from whom he had learnt the science of archery. The Princes then went and narrated the whole episode to Drona, their teacher. Drona remembered the hunter- lad who had asked to be admitted to his school but was denied admission. Drona immediately summoned the young Gorodus from the forest.

Drona asked the boy, "Young man, how does it happen that you are my disciple?"

Gorodus said, "My Lord, I am your disciple and have learnt everything through your blessing." Drona then said, "In that case, are you ready to pay me the fees that you owe me?" Gorodus was greatly pleased as he was finally accepted as a student and was ready to pay any fees that the master asked him. Drona said, "I want your right thumb as my fee." Without hesitation,

Gorodus, at once cut off his right thumb and presented it to the master. With the loss of the right thumb, Gorodus was forever unable to use his skill in archery. Trilock would become the best archer without Gorodus! This would fulfill Drona's promise to Godash that Trilock would be the best archer in the world.

After some time, Drona wanted to test his students in the art of archery. He thus fixed a clay model of a bird on a branch of a tree and asked the princes to take aim at the bird. Vilmaril was the first to be asked.

Drona said, "Son, look carefully at me, then at the tree, then at the target and then take aim." "What do you see?" asked Drona. Vilmaril replied, "I see you, I see the tree and the target." Drona told Vilmaril to stand aside. Assura was the next but he, too, was disqualified as he gave the same reply. The other princes also repeated the same answer. Drona was not happy with their reply. Finally, it was the turn of Trilock.

Drona said Trilock, "What do you see?"

Trilock said, "I see the bird."

Drona said, "What else do you see?"

Trilock replied, "I see the head of the bird."

Drona again asked, "What else do you see?"

Trilock was so engrossed in looking at the bird that he made no reply.

Drona shouted loudly, "Shoot."

Immediately the head of the bird was pierced through by the flight of an arrow. Trilock's power of concentration was excellent and he had mastered the art of archery.

On another occasion, Drona had gone to the river Urila for a bath when a crocodile caught his leg. The other disciples were bewildered and did not know what to do. Only Trilock had presence of mind and he shot several arrows to cut the crocodile into pieces. Drona was very pleased with Trilock and taught him about the most powerful weapon, called "Thunderborn," which he could use in extreme cases and especially against demons and gods.

THE BIRTH OF THE SON OF
THE SUN-GOD:

After her union with the sun god, Noralius had given birth to Karna whom she put in a basket and floated it in the river Urila. A charioteer named Goralis happened to see this basket while bathing in the river. He took the baby home and he and his wife were extremely happy to have the lovely baby. They named the boy Karna, which means son of the charioteer.

As the boy grew up, he had no desire to become a charioteer but wanted to learn the martial arts. He went to seek admission to the archery school at Hastin. However, Drona denied him admission, just as he had earlier done to Gorodus, as he was only a son of a charioteer and only a commoner. Karna was disappointed but was not disheartened.

He had heard of the well-known sage, Lukotos, and decided to become his disciple. Sage Lukotos was not very fond of the Warrior class so Karna presented himself before him as a commoner. He was readily accepted and soon became the favorite of the master, so much so that the master even taught him to use the Wind-Fire weapon.

Once, while sage Lukotos wanted to have siesta in the afternoon, he rested his head on the lap of his favorite disciple. Just at that time an insect stung the thigh of Karna and blood started oozing out. There was excruciating pain in his thigh. Karna did not want to disturb the sleep of his master so he bore the pain. Soon the warm blood began to flow on the face of the master and he woke up. Sage Lukotos wondered where the blood came from and then came to know from Karna about the sting of the insect. "How could a commoner bear such a lot of pain? Only a warrior has the capacity to undergo such pain." "Tell me the truth." He asked Karna. "Are you a warrior or a commoner?" Now Karna could not hide the truth. He fell at the feet of the master and revealed his identity. He begged pardon of the master.

Sage Lukotos was furious and was not ready to show any mercy. To him class was of the utmost importance. He cursed his beloved disciple saying, "When you are in utmost need, your memory will fail and you will not be able to use the weapons since you have tried to deceive me." Very frustrated, Karna returned to his foster parents.

At Hastin, Drona was eager to arrange a competition among all his students and to exhibit their talents. Therefore he asked permission of Godash and Lohas who readily agreed. Soon a day was fixed. Drona, Kripa and Ashwa entered the stage first and were honored by the king. Then followed all the other princes.

There was a mace duel between Assura and Hugo. It was becoming so dangerous that Ashwa had to intervene and separate the two warriors. All these proceedings were narrated to Lohas, the blind king, by Vidura and to Wardoria, who still wore the bandage over her eyes to honor her husband, by Noralius.

Then came Trilock, the ace archer, who performed various skills of archery and thrilled everyone. Suddenly there was a great uproar and a loud sound. All eyes turned in that direction when they saw mighty Karna entering the arena. After getting permission from Drona, Karna displayed all the brilliance of archery, which he had mastered from his guru, sage Lukotos. All were tongue-tied and Trilock felt humbled.

All eyes were now on Karna. Noralius saw that the new comer was wearing the Sun ring, the royal symbols that he had when he was born. She at once recognized him to be Karna, her secret son out of wedlock, and almost swooned. It was only Vidura who, with his special boon, could understand the full implication of the situation. Karna then challenged Trilock to a single duel between them. Just then, Kripa stepped in and asked the lineage of the stranger because, as he said, commoners were not allowed to challenge the royalty. Karna did not know what to say.

Seeing the sad plight of the stranger, Assura, the eldest of the hundred Telhoth brothers, stepped in and defended Karna, saying that one can become a king also by bravery, not only by birth or conquest. It is our prerogative to crown him king of Martyl, a country that so far has no king. Thus, Karna was made king and included in the ranks of the princes.

Exactly at this time there appeared in the stadium an old man. Karna at once recognized him to be his foster father, Goralis, and, falling at his feet, he asked his blessings. Now everyone came to believe that Karna was a commoner. He was spurned by all except Noralius who recognized him to be the son of the Sun-God but could not reveal it to any one.

Assura again came to Karna's rescue by saying that class was not the most important factor. Many famous sages and kings did not belong to the warrior class, and yet they rose to great heights. Karna should be allowed to compete with Trilock, argued Assura. During those days there was a rule that all activities of a martial nature must stop at sunset. As sunset was drawing close, the tournament ended and every one retired from the field. Karna thought that he had lost a chance to prove his ability. He remained bitter about it.

ARCHERY TEACHER AND HIS CHILDHOOD FRIEND:

Drona could not forget the humiliation that he had received from his boyhood friend, King Anga of Angus, and wished to avenge that insult some day. As the training of the princes was almost over, he thought of demanding tuition fees from his students. He urged the princes to invade the kingdom of Angus and defeat King Anga. The Prols were a little hesitant to take part in this venture, but the Telhoths were eager and they invaded Angus without the Prols. However, King Anga defeated the Telhoths with the help of his brother. Just then, Trilock intervened and, charging on King Anga, they carried him captive to Drona.

Drona was elated, as his plan had finally succeeded. Drona reminded King Anga of the humiliation that he had caused him, but he showed him mercy and returned half his kingdom. King Anga was touched by this magnanimity, embraced Drona lovingly, and was thus reconciled with him.

ᛒILMARIL, ᛏHE ᛕROWN ᛈRINCE:

ᛒhen Vilmaril was of the proper age, he was appointed the crown prince. Lohas did not favor this. He wanted to crown his own son, Assura, king. Godash, Vidura and Drona, however, wished to appoint Vilmaril the king since he was the eldest and was endowed with all the noble virtues befitting a king. They argued that the throne actually belonged to King Prol, the father of five Prol brothers who would have been the king if he was in good health and had not retired to the forest. Lohas was only a substitute king replacing King Prol and so Assura was not the rightful heir but Vilmaril was as he was the son of the King Prol. The cousins were not very happy but could not protest. They all mutually agreed that Vilmaril should be made king temporarily and his performance as a king should be reviewed. Soon after his appointment, Vilmaril proved his worth. He had all the virtues required of a king, became very popular, and was even able to expand his kingdom.

In the meantime, Hugo and Assura became the pupils of Rahul, the elder brother of Mohan, and learnt from him the art of mace wielding to perfection. Trilock too progressed further in the art of archery and was considered next only to Mohan, the god.

The common topic discussed among the people was about the future king. Lohas was feeble and blind while Godash had renounced the throne. Thus, the only person fit to be the king was Vilmaril. The ever-ambitious Assura was uncomfortable with this view and complained about this to his father, Lohas. The father, however, cautioned him against any hasty step, advised him to consult Kanika, a minister with Sakuni, as he was a very learned man and well versed in worldly wisdom.

They consulted Kanika, a shrewd minister trusted by Lohas, in secret and asked for his advice. After pondering the matter, Kanika gave the following advice to Assura. "Try to pretend outwardly that you are very fond of the Prols, but hide your secret hatred for them. Let them not know your inner feelings at any time."

Assura then revealed a secret plot to his father, "Please send the Prols along with their mother Noralius for a change to a distant place like Solmin and let them spend a year there. In the meanwhile, I will try to strengthen my position here. I will see to it that they do not return to Hastin." Lohas agreed to this suggestion.

Secretly encouraged by Assura, the ministers began to sing praises of the place called Solmin and the soothing effect it would produce on the Prols. In fact, Lohas summoned all the Prols personally and spoke to them about the merits of an outing to Solmin and how it would recuperate them physically and mentally.

So, thoughtlessly, Vilmaril agreed to this suggestion and decided to go to Solmin after taking leave of Godash, Vidura and Drona. Some citizens saw in this a sinister plot of the Telhoths, but Vilmaril pacified them by saying that no harm would come to them. Only Vidura, who had a premonition of a coming disaster, accompanied them up to a certain distance and warned them of a possible plot or an accident. He also reminded them how, during a fire, rats burrow holes into the ground to escape the fire. After giving this advice, Vidura returned home and the Prols reached the place called Solmin.

THE WICKED "HOUSE OF WAX" PLOT:

A ssura was happy that the Prols had finally reached Solmin and now he could carry out the plot with the help of Sakuni, his uncle. Sakuni appointed one of his crafty ministers, Purolius, to accomplish the task. For this purpose, he decided to build a grand mansion in the forest, of flammable materials like lac, resin, wax that could easily catch fire. The Prols would be burnt alive in this mansion and no one would come to know about it.

The people of Solmin were too happy to welcome the arrival of the royal entourage of the Prols in their midst and gave them a royal welcome. Soon the new mansion was ready with a huge moat around it and the Prols were invited to occupy it. So the Prols came to stay in the new mansion. Vilmaril and Hugo quickly realized that there was something suspicious about the mansion and that it was a death trap. In the meantime, Vidura, who had the ability to see the future, sent an expert miner to Solmin and told him to dig a secret tunnel from the wax house to the nereby forest. While the Prols were engaged in hunting along with Purolios, the work of building the tunnel continued.

Purolious fixed a day for setting the house on fire. A few days before this Vidura had alerted the Prols about the plot and the danger. One day Noralius arranged for a grand party in which Purolius and his friends were supplied with good food and drink and were soon fast asleep. At midnight, the brothers along with their mother, crawled through the secret tunnel. Hugo set the mansion on fire and escaped at the end. The burning material covered the tunnel so that no one could know anything. Thus, the Prols escaped safely to the forest.

As the fire raged, the people of Solmin could see from far off that the mansion was completely gutted and suspected some foul play by Assura and his father. When they looked at the burnt bones and ashes, they took it for granted that the Prols were burnt alive. Actually, the remains they found were those of Purolius and all his friends.

The sad news of the Prols reached Hastin and while the Telhoths were full of glee, Godash and Vidura were subdued and controlled their emotions.

THE DEMON IS KILLED:

After escaping from the House of Wax, the Prols reached the forest on the southern part of the river Urila. Noralius was very thirsty and longed for water. So Hugo set out in search of water. There was a lake close by with pure and clear water. As he approached the lake, he saw a very enchanting lady. He asked her who she was. She replied that she was Deolana, the sister of Hidimba, the demon. "My brother ordered me to kill all of you since we, being demons, are fond of human flesh. But looking at your pleasing personality I have fallen in love with you. Please accept me."

But Hugo rejected all her advances and told her that without the permission of his mother and brothers he would have nothing to do with her.

This annoyed Deolana. Back at home, Hidimba was getting more and more anxious as Deolana was late. He rushed to the spot where Hugo and Deolana were conversing and at once charged at Hugo. There was a terrible duel between the two, the sound of which awoke all the other Prols and Noralius. Trilock joined in the fight but Hugo alone was a match for Hidimba as he lifted him high above the ground and turning him round and round several times finally threw him onto the ground where he lay dead.

Deolana, however, followed the Prols as she was greatly enamoured of Hugo and wanted to marry him. She pleaded with Noralius to allow her to marry Hugo and promised them all possible help. Taking pity on her and with the consent of Vilmaril, she allowed Hugo to get married to Deolana. Both of them lived together till a son was born to them whom they named Fioril, the pot-headed. Hugo eventually had to separate from Deolana to carry on his worldy duties and after taking Deolana's concent left the forest. Deolana was more than happy for the separation as she understood that Hugo was a human after all and that he belonged to the world of humans.

HUGO ENCOUNTERS THE WICKED GIANT.

The sage Yasa, who was keeping in constant touch with the Prols, exhorted them to bear the present sorrows bravely and advised them to go to Mt. Apex a forrest area and stay there. The Prols remained in hiding for a few months so that Telhoths would think that they were dead and in the meantime the Prols would remain safe and plan their next strategy. The Prols came to the Mt.Apex and resided with a commoner. Though they behaved like mendicants, people felt that their behavior was that of royals.

Once Noralius heard wailing and weeping in the house and asked the cause of it. They then explained that a certain wicked giant, called Baka, was spreading terror among the citizens, as he daily wanted not only food and drink but also a human as a meal. The citizens had agreed to send one human daily according to turn. That day happened to be the turn of that family and the members were vying with one another to offer themselves to the Baka.

Hearing this sad story, Noralius was ready to send one of her sons to Baka as sacrifice but the host would not listen. Noralius told them that no harm would come to any of her sons since the gods were protecting them. Hugo volunteered to go to challenge the giant. He took a cartload of food and purposely reached the dwelling of Baka late, which annoyed the giant.

As Baka came out, he saw Hugo feasting on the sumptuous food that he had carried for the giant. This infuriated the giant and he rushed at Hugo. There was violent tussle, but Hugo proved too strong for Baka and soon tore the giant into pieces. Thus Mt. Apex was rid of the cruel giant, Baka.

THE ARCHERY COMPETION:

Once, as the Prols were conversing with a wandering man, they came to know about princess Arywiel and about the marriage that King Anga of Angus had arranged for her daughter. Originally, the king had intended to give his daughter to Trilock but he was saddened by the events in the wax house. Still he wished that Trilock were alive and hoped that he would make his appearance at the marriage.

Hearing this, the Prols decided to go to the marriage in disguise. Sage Yasa appeared to them and blessed them with every success in this mission. Thus, they proceeded to Kampilya, the capital of Angus.

THE PRINCESS'S MARRIAGE:

There were great preparations at Angus with all the important princes from far and wide being invited, including the Telhoths. The Prols came to the city secretly and stayed with a potter in the poor part of the city. They moved among the crowds pretending to be commoners.

The day for the marriage dawned, and the whole town was full of gaiety with decorations everywhere and melodious music resonating in every street. In the royal hall, Arywiel sat dressed in the most beautiful attire and drawing the attention of one and all. After escorting her to the centre of the stage, Jorulo, her brother made the following announcement, "Respected Kings, princes and honorable citizens, high up above the lake there is the target, a fish that is revolving about at a great speed on a pole. There is a big circular pond below where you can see the reflection of the fish. Here is the bow and arrow. You have to aim at the moving fish by looking at its reflection in the water. Whoever is able to hit the fish in the eye will marry my sister."

Some of the kings and princes tried their hand at the bow and arrow but were unsuccessful. Assura attempted with great skill but narrowly missed the target. Then came Karna, whose performance was superb but he too could not hit the target. When all the kings and princes had failed, Arywiel's brother announced that the contest was now open to the gentry, i.e. the common people belonging to any class. A young commoner got up, walked up to the centre with royal demeanor and picked up the bow and arrow. All eyes turned to that direction. In silence they looked at him. Stringing the bow, he took up an arrow, looked at the reflection of the fish in the water and, with full concentration, let go the arrow. The arrow pierced the eye of the fish. There was resounding applause from every corner of the royal hall and everyone gave the young commoner a standing ovation.

Walking gracefully like a swan, Arywiel went up to the stranger and garlanded him with the a nuptial garland, while there was the sound of music and showering of petals on the newly married couple. King Angus felt happy that he had such a handsome son-in-law.

TRILOCK MARRIES PRINCESS ARYWIEL:

After the marriage ceremony, the Prols and Noralius returned to their humble dwelling. As they entered the house they shouted with one voice, "Mother, look at what, we have brought for you today." Without looking at Arywiel, Noralius replied, "All of you may share the gift." But when she saw Arywiel, she realized her mistake (In those days a word or a command from the mother had to be respected by all means even if the words were uttered by mistake). But the Prols consoled her by saying that all the five of them would share the gift equally and so Arywiel became the wife of all the five Prols. Arywiel's brother, who had accompanied the Prols, now came to know that the poor commoners were, in fact, the five Prols, supposed to have been burnt alive in the House of Wax. And the lady was their mother, Noralius. News of the Prols soon spread everywhere.

ᴛHE ᴄITY ᴏF ᴊLLUSION: ᴚOSHUK

odash, Vidura and the common people were happy to hear the news of the Prols' miraculous escape and about Trilock's exceptional feat. But Lohas, Assura, Karna and other Telhoths were greatly perturbed by this unexpected happening. They at once invaded the kingdom of Angus but they met with a defeat. In the meantime Godash, Vidura and Drona met with Lohas and persuaded him to invite the Prols back to Hastin and advised him to divide the kingdom between the two groups so that they could live in peace and harmony.

Lohas was moved by this suggestion and agreed to bring the Prols back to Hastin. And thus the Prols came back to Hastin along with Noralius and Arywiel. It was Mohan, Noralius cousin brother, who accompanied the brothers back. Shortly, Vilmaril was crowned the king and was advised to go to Roshuk, the ruined capital. Though the place was not fertile and well developed, Vilmaril willingly moved there along with all his brothers and family members while the Telhoths remained in Hastin.

This new place was soon developed into a beautiful capital city. After this, Mohan took leave of all and retired to Port Aigcatlos.

At this juncture, Narad, the great sage, appeared on the scene and gave a piece of advice to the Prols regarding Arywiel so that they would not quarrel among themselves. They would, in turn, act as the husbands to Arywiel for one year each.

TRILOCK MARRIES PRINCESS SIRIL:

After this incident Trilock took leave of them all and proceeded on a pilgrimage for a year. He wandered all over the country and reached the place called Pratukos. Mohan who was keeping a close watch on Trilock and his movements had come to know that his own sister, Siril, was secretly in love with Trilock. Mohan reached Pratukos in disguise and took Trilock to Port Aigcatlos where Siril was to serve Trilock and thus win his heart. This plan worked well Trilock fell in love with Siril and soon he planned to marry her. Mohan, who knew everything, was delighted and Siril was married to Trilock in a grand ceremony.

In due time, Siril gave birth to a boy, whom they named Liran and who grew up to be a virtuous young man. At Hastin, Arywiel, in turn, gave birth to five sons who grew up to be fine young men.

THE EXILE:

THE END OF JARALUZ:

Since Trilock had helped him, Maya thought it to be his duty to reciprocate and help the Prols build the assembly hall, as he was an able architect. Maya went far and wide to bring the best materials for the construction of the hall and within fourteen months, the wonderful hall was built. Narad was so impressed by the architecture of the hall that he proposed to perform a "Victory Ceremony" to prove the Prols' superiority over all the other kings and princes.

Some people objected to this proposal but Mohan was in favor of it. The chief opposition came from King Jaraluz of Magadha. Jaraluz, who was a very cruel monarch, had captured very many kings and had kept them as captives. So Magadha was invaded and Jaraluz was killed. All the captive kings were liberated. The "Victory Ceremony" was finally performed with great pomp and pageantry. Mohan was the chief guest on this auspicious occasion, which some of the visitors did not like. The foremost among them was Sisupala who ridiculed Mohan and called him all sorts of names to insult him. It was then that Mohan was forced to use his wheel-weapon with which he severed the head of Sisupala. The wheel-weapon was rarely used by Mohan and that only in extreme cases. This was a devine weapon which only a god could use. The weapon had the power to annihilate the entire earth.

The ceremony was finally performed with all the rituals and festivities. Thus Vilmaril became the emperor with superiority over all the other kings.

The Telhoths and the other kings were greatly impressed by the grandeur of the palace, built by Maya. In fact, Assura, Sakuni and Karna stayed back when the others had departed after the inauguration, since they wanted to inspect the palace closely. At several places in the palace they were fooled by the numerous optical illusions which Maya had created and which baffled them. Once, while Hugo was walking Assura through the palace, they came across a swimming pool which Assura mistook for a floor of glass and tried to walk on, but he fell into the pool, which made Arywiel laugh loudly from the window. She shouted loudly, poking fun at Assura by crying, "Son of a blind is a blind too ". Assura was furious that Arywiel insulted him and his father and decided to take revenge some day.

The Telhoth brothers jealousy was unbearable and they were bent on revenge but did not know how to go about it. Telhoths knew that they could never win against Prols in conventional warfare. The only way open to them was by some treachery or craft that they could use to vanquish the Prols and quench their vengeance. The crafty Sakuni then came up with the superb idea of gambling or a game of dice in which they could deceive Vilmaril who had a weakness of playing dice game and win back their empire. Assura liked this idea and supported it whole heartedly. The blind king did not like the idea but finally gave his consent. Vidura, too, was unwilling at first but agreed to go to Roshuk to invite the

Prols to the newly built hall for a game of dice. It was not uncommon in those days for kings and princes to play dice as a sport. But Vilmaril suspected some treachery in this proposition as he was not at all good in this sport while Sakuni and others were past masters in the game. However, he could not refuse, and the day was fixed for the contest.

THE GAME OF DICE:

So the game began. Vilmaril asked, "Who plays the game and what is the wager?" Assura replied, "My uncle Sakuni plays the game for me while I will wager whatever we decide." Though this was not fair, Vilmaril agreed upon it. All the spectators including Godash, Vidura, Kripa, Drona and others were eagerly watching the game.

Then Vilmaril announced, "In the first wager, I bet all my gold, jewels and gems." Assura also wagered all his valuables. Sakuni tossed the dice and cast it on the floor. Loudly he shouted, "Here, I have won." So Vilmaril had to part with all his jewels. Then came the second wager, in which Vilmaril bet all his possessions, but within no time he lost that too with the cunning trickery of Sakuni. The next bet for the Roshuk Empire. Vidura was getting extremely agitated and impatient at the treachery of the Telhoths but was spurned by Assura and Sakuni. Vilmaril now could not control himself and wanted to wager more and more. The Prol brothers were the next bet. One by one he lost them too.

At this juncture, Assura and Sakuni remembered the defeat and insult that they had suffered at the hands of the Prols in the marriage ceremony of Arywiel at Angus. Now was their chance to avenge that insult. So they demanded that Arywiel should be wagered now that the Prols had lost everything. Everyone was aghast to hear this. Never in their wildest dreams had the Prols ever imagined such a situation. The outcome was obvious. Vilmaril lost Arywiel in the last bet.

The Telhoths were jubilant and Assura's and Sakuni's joy knew no bounds. With a thunder, Sakuni ordered his brother Amon to drag Arywiel and bring her to the hall. They fetched Arywiel and she was made to stand before everyone in utter humiliation. She begged Vilmaril and others to save her honor, but they were all cast down and dejected, incapable of doing anything. Amon was asked to strip Arywiel of her dress so she would be ridiculed before all.

Just then Arywiel remembered Mohan, the god who had earlier helped the Prols in their moment of crisis. She fervently prayed to Mohan and pleaded with him to save her honor. And Mohan did come to her rescue. Amon began to strip Arywiel yard by yard. But the dress seemed to be stretching longer and longer. He pulled and pulled with all his might but there seemed to be no end to it and the heap of cloth went on rising into a mountain. Amon was finally exhausted and fell down unconscious. Seeing this wonderful miracle, all were aghast. Arywiel's honor had been saved.

ᴛHE ᴮLIND ᴷING ᴵNTERVENES:

ᵂhen Lohas learned of this strange occurrence, his soul was moved, and he could not restrain himself any longer. He immediately summoned Arywiel and spoke to her thus, "My child, I am sorry to hear what has happened to you. I wish to undo the wrong that my sons have caused you. Ask for any boon you wish and it shall be granted."

Then bowing low, Arywiel asked for the life of Vilmaril, which was granted to her without any hesitation. Again he said to her, "Ask for another boon." So she said, "Let all the other Prols be freed." Lohas agreed to this too. And he asked her once more, "Ask for one more boon and it be given to you." But Arywiel remained silent. Then Lohas on his own gave back to the Prols their kingdom, Roshuk, and told them to go back there and live in peace.

Hardly had the Prols reached their kingdom when Assura and others conferred with the blind king and persuaded him not to trust the Prols. In fact, they suggested that they be banished into the Banjara forest for twelve years. "Let us play one more game of dice," they said. "If the Prols lose this time, they should be sent to the forest for twelve years and they must spend one more year in disguise and hiding." Lohas as desperate as he was to protect Assura was convinced of this step and agreed to go ahead with this plan.

So the Prols were called back and forced to play one more game of dice. The crafty Sakuni, this time too, managed to manipulate the dice and deceive the Prols. The Prols lost one more round of the game. Now they were left with no other option. They had to go to the Banjara forest for twelve long years and had to spend one more year in hiding. If they were discovered during this time of concealment, they would be forced to extend the forest stay for another twelve years. Assura and the Telhoths were delighted to hear this verdict of the blind king. They thought that this would be the end of the Prols. The Telhoths were, now, the supreme authority over both the kingdoms of Hastin and Roshuk. The verdict again proved the desperation of Lohas to make his son Assura the supreme ruler of Hastin and Roshuk. The Prols took the verdict gracefully.

In Banjara Forest:

T rue to his word, Vilmaril accepted the verdict of Lohas, his uncle, and proceeded to the Banjara forest with all his brothers and Arywiel. Life in the forest was not easy but the Prols had made up their minds to live like ascetics and so they were satisfied with their frugal life style. Their real problem was when guests came to visit them, as many did, to see how they lived and what sufferings they underwent. To fulfill their own needs and the needs of the visitors, Vilmaril prayed to the Sun-god to help them in their time of difficulty. The Sun-god heard his prayers and gifted him a miraculous vessel. The cooked food was to be placed in this vessel and the food would remain inexhaustible for the day. This satisfied the needs of the Prols and especially of the ever-hungry Hugo.

Once the famous sage Zykos paid a visit to them in the forest along with hundreds of his followers. Meal time was over and Arywiel did not know what to do, as the divine vessel would produce food only twice a day, once in the morning and once in the evening. Arywiel then remembered Mohan and prayed to him to help her in this crisis. Mohan appeared on the scene and asked Arywiel to show him the vessel.

He saw that there was one grain of rice still left in the vessel. He ate up that grain and felt as if he had a complete meal. When he came out to meet sage Zykos and his men, they, too, felt as if they had a full meal without putting even a grain in their mouth. Sage Zykos at once realized that it was the work of Mohan and blessed Arywiel for it.

During the Prols' stay in the Banjara forest, as earlier mentioned, a number of visitors came to meet them and inquire about their well being. Among the first one was Vidura who informed the Prols of the sad state of affairs at Hastin where people were not at all happy with the Telhoths and particularly with Assura and his rule. Assura was suspicious of Vidura's visits to the Banjara forest and so he was plotting to kill the Prols in exile so that they would never be a problem to the Telhoths. It was only the intervention of sage Yasa which prevented this step.

ꞮHE ꞂOW:

Ꙇ mong the others who visited the Prols in the forest was the sage Maitlucos. He was shocked to learn about the wickedness of the Telhoths, especially that of Assura and the silence of Lohas. He comforted the Prols and consoled them by saying that the final victory would be theirs.

Mohan was the next to visit the Prols in the forest. He went along with other relatives to search for the Prols in the Banjara forest. When they reached there, they were saddened to see the sad plight of the Prols and Arywiel. Arywiel narrated in detail the ignominy that she had to suffer at the hands of the Telhoths. Mohan then solemnly promised that the Telhoths would not go unpunished and that all the humiliations inflicted on her would be avenged. Arywiel was particularly hurt by the submissive and cowardly behavior of Vilmaril. The other Prols defended Arywiel in this view. But Vilmaril had only one argument that he had to obey and respect his uncle, Lohas, come what may.

$\mathfrak{J}$N $\mathcal{Q}$UEST $\mathfrak{G}$F $\mathfrak{B}$IVINE $\mathcal{W}$EAPONS $\mathfrak{J}$N $\mathfrak{H}$ORODUS $\mathfrak{M}$OUNTAINS:

$\mathfrak{D}$uring this time, sage Yasa paid a visit to the Prols and informed them of the situation in Hastin, how the Telhoths were preparing themselves for a possible war. He advised the Prols to prepare themselves by acquiring knowledge of all kinds of weaponry and the latest methods of warfare. He also suggested that they should look for possible allies and friends who would help them in the event of a war after the period of exile. This was the ideal time for them to make such preparations. Trilock therefore went beneath the surface of the Earth in the Horodus Mountains in quest of divine weapons and underwent severe penance to propitiate the god Siva. Siva was placated and gave him the "Earth Weapon" and the other gods also presented him with divine weapons.

Trilock mastered the use of the various celestial weapons under the able guidance of Erasena, the expert in the use of celestial weapons. At the end of the training, Erasena wanted to test his disciple. So he sent

63

a beautiful lady, Urvasi, to tempt him but Trilock was firm and did not give in to the enticements of the lady. This annoyed Urvasi and she cursed Trilock, saying that he would be a eunuch and a dancer. Erasena, however, intervened and forced Urvasi to limit the curse only to one year which he could use to his advantage during the time of hiding in the thirteenth year.

THE PILGRIMAGE:

The Prols were worried about the long absence of Trilock but the sage Lomasha who visited them informed them that Trilock was doing well in the Horodus Mountains and had mastered all the difficult war strategy and weapons. He would return to the forest shortly. He also suggested the idea of the Prols going on a countrywide pilgrimage. Vilmaril was pleased with this suggestion and the Prols readied themselves to go on a countrywide pilgrimage to all the sacred places. When they were at Port Aigcatlos, Mohan learned about it and he, along with his brother Rahul, visited them and discussed all the matters related to their exile, Trilock's stay at Horodus mountains and the visits of various sages. From here they proceeded to Kailash, the holiest of places.

Encounter With a Monkey:

During their wanderings in the mountains, Arywiel once smelled the sweet, alluring fragrance of a flower. She could not make out where the fragrance was coming from, so she asked Hugo to investigate and locate the flower. Hugo at once set out searching for the rare flower, tearing apart every creeper and shrub on his way. Suddenly, he came upon a huge monkey slumbering happily among the plantain groves. Hugo tried to wake the giant monkey who was fast asleep. It finally woke up and chided Hugo for disturbing him in his sleep. As the monkey was blocking Hugo's way, he asked the monkey to move aside and make way for him. Hugo did not want to cross over the body of the giant monkey. However, the monkey told Hugo very politely to lift his tail a little and make way for himself. Hugo at once tried to lift the tail to put it aside. To his great surprise he found that he could not move the tail even a little bit.

Hugo at once understood that this was not any ordinary monkey. So he asked him, "Please tell me who you are!" The monkey replied that he was Hanumana, the son of the wind god. Hugo was happy and told the monkey that he, too, was the son of the wind god and Noralius. Both embraced each other and Hanumana, the monkey, bestowed a boon on Hugo, saying that he would reside on the flagstaff of Trilock's chariot in the war against the Telhoths. He also showed him the exact location where he could find the fragrant flower for Arywiel. Soon all the Prols were reunited, including Trilock who came down from Horodus Mountain. Trilock narrated all his adventures in the mountains and his acquisition of the knowledge of the divine weapons.

In this way ten years of forest life passed and the Prols decided to spend the last two years in the Banjara forest where they had begun their exile.

ᴀSSURA ᴊS ᴋUMILIATED:

ᴊ̶F̶ ar away at Hastin, Assura's heart burned with jealousy, particularly when reports of the Prols reached him. A certain commoner visited Hastin and related to Lohas and all the other Telhoths how the Prols were growing not only in wisdom, virtue and forbearance but also thay they had acquired the highest knowledge of warfare and Trilock had mastered the use of the celestial weapons from the gods. He told them that the Prols, far from being unhappy and suffering, were becoming stronger by the day with the visits of Mohan, sage Yasa, the sages and even gods. So Karna, Sakuni and Assura conferred and decided to attack the Prols in the forest where they were unarmed and unprotected and thus destroy them completely. Lohas also agreed to this suggestion. They wondered, however, what excuse to give for this sudden attack on the Prols.

Assura then suggested to them the idea of visiting their cattle farm and dairy in the forest, which was liked by one and all. So Assura and his companions set out for the forest where the Prols lived. No sooner did they enter the boundary of the forest than the local people who were well wishers of Prols attacked them under the leadership of King Chitrasena. Assura's army was thoroughly defeated and Assura himself was taken captive while Karna and Sakuni managed to flee. Assura and the Telhoth captives were produced before Vilmaril. The righteous Vilmaril could not see his own cousins in chains and at once ordered them to be released. Utterly humiliated and full of shame, Assura returned to Hastin, but was unable to forget the bitter sting he had received at the hands of the King Chitrasena.

THE VICTORY CEREMONY:

Assura, Karna and Sakuni were constantly conferring and planning various plots to thwart any attempt by the Prols to overpower them or to look superior to them. In this context, Assura could not forget the "Victory Ceremony" performed by the Prols which had glorified them and caused them to be held in high esteem by gods and eminent men. He thought that he should also perform such a ceremony to which he proposed to invite the Prols. He dispatched emissaries to the forest to invite them to the ceremony, but the Prols declined the offer saying that they were bound by conditions imposed on them for thirteen years and so could not attend such a ceremony.

The date for the ceremony was finally fixed and all the kings and princes were invited. The ceremony was performed with all the rituals and ceremonies befitting such an occasion. All the invitees were very much impressed by the grandeur of the ceremony and were all praise for Assura and his friends. Karna, on this solemn occasion, also took a vow to seek vengeance on the Prols and swore that he would abstain from meat and drink and would lead a life of an ascetic till he had vanquished the Prols.

THE MYSTERIOUS HAUNTED LAKE:

Twelve long years of forest life were coming to an end. Once, while trying to help a commoner who was in trouble, the Prols happened to be lost in the forest. They were filled with terrible thirst and wanted water. Vilmaril asked Nakula to go in search of water and bring some to him as he was dying of thirst. Nakula at once set out in search of water. Shortly he came to a lovely lake with crystal clear water. He was very happy. "Let me first quench my thirst and then I will carry water for my brothers," he said to himself. Hardly did he bend to take a sip of water when he heard a strange voice saying, "This Lake belongs to me. First answer my questions and then drink the water." Nakula was so overcome with thirst that he had no patience to answer the questions of the invisible speaker and he at once bent down to drink the water. As soon as he took a sip of water, he fell down dead.

The other brothers were waiting eagerly for Nakula to return since they, too, were dying of thirst. When Nakula did not return, Shakula volunteered to go and look for Nakula and bring water for the other brothers. He set out and soon he came to the beautiful lake where he saw his dear brother Nakula lying dead. He was infuriated but wanted to quench his thirst first. So he bent down to take a sip of water.

Then he heard a voice, "Don't drink this water before answering my questions. This lake is mine. If you drink the water before answering my questions you will die like your brother who is lying dead here." But Shakula also had no patience to answer the questions. He was very eager to drink the water and immediately bent down to drink the water, and he, too, fell down dead on the spot.

Then came the turn of Trilock who soon came to the lake and saw his dear brothers lying dead. He found no marks of injury on their bodies and wondered how the brothers died. But first and foremost he wanted to satisfy his thirst so he bent down to reach the water. Thereupon he heard a strange voice, "Don't touch the water. If you don't wish to die as your brothers died, answer my questions first and then drink the water." But Trilock also could not control himself and entered the lake and began to drink the water. Immediately he also fell down dead.

Next came the turn of Hugo. He set out in search of his brothers and came to the lake where he was horrified to see the dead bodies of his dear brothers. He wondered what had happened and who had killed his brothers. But he wanted to quench his thirst first before anything else. He had entered the lake when he heard a strange voice saying, "Hugo, don't drink this water or else you will meet the same fate as your brothers. Answer my questions first and then drink from the lake."

Hugo did not know who it was that spoke but without answering any questions, he took the water of the lake in his palms and began to drink. He died on the spot at once.

Greatly troubled by the disappearance of all his brothers, Vilmaril did not know what to do. As he could not bear the pang of thirst, he went in search of water and came to the lake. When he saw his brothers dead, he could not bear his sorrow. He cursed himself for sending his brothers in search of water. He wondered how he could face his mother and Arywiel. But the same voice beckoned him saying, "Vilmaril, you see your brothers dead because they did not heed my advice. You, too, will face the same fate if you do not answer my questions before drinking this water."

Vilmaril realized that the voice was the voice of a Yaksha, the lake spirit, and he said to it, "I know that this lake belongs to you. I have no right to drink this water. I am ready to answer your questions."

The invisible voice asked several questions about parents, happiness, virtues and vices. Vilmaril answered them all so well that the voice was pleased and said to Vilmaril, "I am fully satisfied with your answers. I will restore all your brothers to you. Tell me whom do you want to be revived first." Vilmaril answered, "Please give me back Nakula first." "Why do you ask for Nakula and not Trilock or Hugo". "Because I am the son of Noralius and am still alive while Madri has no son as both her sons are dead." The voice was pleased by this magnanimous reply of Vilmaril and it revived all the brothers. Vilmaril was puzzled by the actions of the strange voice and asked, "Please tell me who you are."

"I am your heavenly father Prol and I am immensely pleased by your righteous conduct. So I revived all your brothers."

Thus, all the brothers came back to life. Vilmaril embraced his heavenly father who blessed him and all the Prols. He promised to look after them in all eventualities. He advised them to go to the King of Fohol for their last year of hiding where they would be able to live incognito and without any problem. So saying, the father disappeared from their sight

☰HE ☰HIRTEENTH 𝒴EAR:

𝔄 ccording to the advice of the heavenly father, the Prols were to spend the thirteenth year with King Viralius of Fohol and stay there in concealment, so that no one would know of their whereabouts. After proper thought and planning, the Prols decided to approach King Viralius of the Fohol kingdom. King Viralius was a powerful and wise king and was respected and feared by all his neighbors.

Without revealing their identity, the Prol brothers and Arywiel journeyed to the Fohol kingdom and approached King Viralius one by one so that no one would suspect them. Vilmaril was the first one to go to the king and volunteered to work as his companion and advisor since he was a nobleman accustomed to such work with the Prols. He also told King Viralius that he was good at playing dice and would entertain the king in that sport. The king was impressed by the noble ways of the gentleman and immediately employed him in his service.

Then came the turn of Hugo. He presented himself as a very good cook, who was expert in all manner of culinary work. He was, besides, a very good wrestler and would delight the king by his skill in wrestling. The king was impressed by the hefty, strong body of Hugo and employed him as a cook.

According to the curse of Urvasi, Trilock was supposed to serve in a royal court as a eunuch in the company of other female servants and so here was a good excuse for Trilock to take up such a job in the court of King Viralius without any danger of his identity being revealed to any one. So Trilock presented himself as a teacher of dance and song and music to the king's daughter Uttara.

Arywiel disguised herself as a servant-maid and flower girl to work in the king's court and as a personal companion to the king's wife. The queen was captivated by the beauty of this young and vivacious lady and promised to keep her in her personal quarters not to be bothered by any one. Arywiel told the queen that she was under the constant protection of the five husbands who had been separated from her for some time.

Nakula was the next to present himself as an expert in looking after the king's horses as he had some experience in this matter. He got employed by the king as the man in charge of the king's stables. Shakula became a cowherd to look after the cattle of the king. Thus all the Prols and Arywiel got employment in King Viralius's kingdom in various capacities as ordinary men though they were all noblemen and warriors.

The first occasion when the Prols had a chance to show their real caliber was the festival of Lord Siva. On this day there was a wrestling match organized among various wrestlers from far and wide. A little-known wrestler challenged all the other wrestlers and defeated them. The king was hurt to see so many of his favorite wrestlers humiliated by this outsider who went on boasting and bragging about his superiority over the others. It was at this time that Kanka reminded the king of the wrestling capacity of the cook, Hugo, and advised the king that he should be persuaded to take on the loudmouth. Hugo was invited to enter the contest which he readily did as this would be the best opportunity for him to show his hidden talent. Hugo entered the arena and challenged the bully. The duel began and in a short time Hugo showed his real talent and thoroughly defeated his opponent. The king was delighted by this and the people cheered the newcomer.

THE SLAYING OF KICHAKA:

ueen of Fohol had a brother named Kichaka, who held the most powerful post of commander-in-chief of the Fohol army. Being the brother-in-law of King Viralius, he enjoyed a special favor with the king and was very powerful. In fact, he held the real power in the Fohol kingdom and various other kings were afraid of him due to his military acumen and harsh ways. The queen had kept Arywiel with her in the inner apartments as she was afraid that the good looks and charming ways of Arywiel might become the source of temptation for many a young man and she would be in danger of losing her chastity.

Almost ten months had passed when on an inauspicious day Kichaka happened to get a glimpse of Arywiel. He was so enamored by the captivating look of Arywiel that he fell in love with her there and then. It was a one-sided love but Kichaka, who was infatuated by the bewitching beauty of the lady, wanted to marry her. He revealed this love to his sister who cautioned him and warned him to remain far from Arywiel as she was constantly protected by her five husbands. But Kichaka failed to see reason and passionately demanded that the maid be handed over to him.

Under the pretext of serving wine to the man, Arywiel was asked to go the chamber of the commander-in-chief. Kichaka at once grabbed the lady in his arms. Arywiel pleaded with him not to take her honor and warned him that her five husbands were looking and protecting her. But Kichaka would not listen to anything. Keeping her presence of mind, Arywiel in a swift movement slipped from Kichaka's grasp and ran out of the chamber to the inner apartments of the queen. There was much furor over this incident, but due to the wise intervention of the queen the matter was suppressed.

Meanwhile, Arywiel secretly met Hugo and acquainted him with her plight. "Please rescue me from this predicament or I'll be forced to commit suicide," was Arywiel's request to Hugo. Hugo therefore suggested a plan. "Pretend that you are ready to submit to the advances of Kichaka and willing to meet him in the dance hall at midnight," he told her. "I will take care of the remaining part."

Kichaka was only too happy to know this. He went looking for Arywiel in the dance hall at night when he saw someone lying hidden on a couch. It was dark in the room and Kichaka could not see the figure clearly.

As he tried to arouse the hidden figure, it pounced on him. Kichaka suspected it to be her husband. The giant began to grapple Kichaka and beat him to a pulp. Kichaka could not resist. He was completely crushed by Hugo and killed.

The next day the news of Kichaka's death spread quickly. People took it for granted that the husbands had protected Arywiel from being dishonored by the proud commander-in-chief. They were glad that the cruel despot was destroyed. But the queen was greatly upset. She had lost her dear brother and knew who the real killer was. She also had an idea about the cause of his death knowing from childhood the avaricious nature of his brother. She asked Arywiel to leave the palace, but Arywiel pleaded with her for one more month as eleven months had already elapsed, promising the queen that her husbands would surely reward her for her kindness some day.

KINGDOM OF FOHOL IS ATTACKED:

T hough the Telhoths knew that the Prols were in their final year of complete anonymity, they were eager to know the Prols' whereabouts and their secret movements. If they could be exposed now, then they would have to undertake another twelve years of exile in the forest which would almost put an end to their dream of ever coming back to Roshuk or regaining their kingdom. So Assura had sent spies and asked them to fan out all over the place to locate where the Prols were, but the spies failed to detect the Prols.

Then Assura learned of the sudden death of Kichaka and the unusual circumstances in which it took place. He found something strange and he also guessed that the so-called husbands of Arywiel were none other than the five Prols, in service with the king of Fohol. He concluded, then, that the best course of action for him was to attack King Viralius and expose the Prols who had taken refuge there. With the death of Kichaka, this work would be all the easier.

Thus Assura contacted Suslos, the king of Trigarta, who was a sworn enemy of King Viralius and explained to him the plot to kill the Prols who were hiding in Fohol's kingdom. Now that Kichaka, the strong man of Fohol, was no more, their work would be easy. Together they attacked the cattle of King Viralius and carried them away. This alerted King Viralius who thought of striking at the enemy but hesitated, as he had lost Kichaka, his able commander-in-chief. However, Kanka intervened and encouraged King Viralius by saying that he was well-versed in warfare and would help against the enemy. Kanka also suggested that the services of Hugo, Nakula and Shakula should be used in this war against King Suslos.

Thus encouraged, King Viralius attacked Suslos. In the fierce battle that ensued, King Viralius was defeated and captured alive. The Fohol army was in disarray and was about to retreat when the four unknown warriors suddenly attacked the Trigarta army. Hugo attacked Suslos like a fierce lion and captured him alive and rescued King Viralius. The enemy army had no other option except to surrender. King Viralius was victorious and was very proud of the four secret warriors who had saved his face.

When Assura heard of King Viralius's success, he had no doubt in his mind that the victory was due to the Prols who, in disguise, had helped King Viralius. He therefore made up his mind to attack King Viralius himself. He attacked the Fohol kingdom from the north and started plundering and looting the Fohol kingdom and carrying away his cattle, gold and farm produce. King Fohol was taken by surprise. There was no one to take on the army of Assura. The only person who was in the court at that time was Kumar, the son of King Viralius who was yet a young lad in his teens.

THE PRINCE GOES INTO THE BATTLE:

he queen mother encouraged Prince Kumar to take charge of the army and go to the battle. "But I need a good charioteer to guide me in the war and I don't have one," he protested. Just then Arywiel said, "This eunuch (Trilock in disguise) who is a good dancer and musician is also a very able charioteer. He will surely be very helpful to you." So Kumar took Trilock as his charioteer and went into battle. When he saw the mighty army of the Telhoths he was frightened and wanted to flee from the battle-field, but the charioteer somehow cheered him up and persuaded him to continue. Then directing the chariot he led the prince to a secret place near the cremation ground where the Prols had hidden the weapons in a hole in a huge tree.

The prince was stunned to see the huge cache of weapons and asked the charioteer who he was and how he had hidden these weapons there. Now Trilock could not hide the truth any more. He revealed the whole truth. He told him that he was Trilock himself and the other four were the Prols in disguise. He told Kumar not to be afraid, as the Prols would surely succeed in the war. Now the prince took heart and was ready to fight in the battle. Trilock started twanging his bow and discharging arrows. The sound of the arrows frightened the enemy. Assura laughed at the inexperienced lad with his womanish charioteer, but the sound of the arrows put fear into him also.

Drona at once understood that this was not an ordinary charioteer. Only Trilock could discharge arrows in this fashion. There was a heated argument between Drona, Karna and Assura. Assura thought that even if it was Trilock, it did not matter as the Prols were now discovered and, according to the condition put forward, they will have to go back to the forest for another twelve years of exile.

Drona, however, was quick to make the calculation and declared that the period of thirteen years had come to a close, and the Prols were on the right path of truth and justice. Even Godash supported this view. Trilock then directed his arrows at the Telhoths and prevented them from advancing. The Telhoths were forced to retreat and go back to Hastin. Trilock and Kumar had won a decisive victory over the Telhoths.

THE PROLS ARE REVEALED:

When Trilock and Prince Kumar returned from the battle, they were given a hero's welcome. King Viralius felt very proud that his young son had shown such gallantry in the war. But the son, who now knew the secret, said to his father, "Father, this charioteer who looks like a eunuch is not a lady but is a Prol warrior. He is Trilock, the great archer in disguise." Then one by one he revealed the true identity of the five Prols and of Arywiel, all of whom were employed in the king's court. "This is Vilmaril, the emperor of Roshuk". King Viralius could not believe his eyes. He thought that Prince Kumar, his son, was the real hero of the battle. Then Kumar introduced Hugo, Nakula and Shakula who were in disguise.

King Viralius was overwhelmed with joy. He embraced Vilmaril and begged forgiveness of him for any rudeness he might have shown him. But Vilmaril replied, "O king, you need not ask for any forgiveness. You have been so noble and kind to employ us in your kingdom and give us shelter. Without your help we would not have been able to pass this last year of concealment undetected. You have saved us from a great calamity."

In the same way, the queen almost knelt before Arywiel and asked pardon of her for any disrespect she might have shown to her in her ignorance. Out of gratitude, the king went so far as to offer his daughter Uttara to Trilock to accept her as his bride. But Trilock was quick to reply, "She is only a child. I am already advanced in age. I have always looked upon her as my daughter." Then, invoking blessings on the young maid, Trilock inwardly said, "Someday a more promising young man will offer his hand to you." He had in mind his own son, Liran born of Siril.

There was much merry making and great festivities in Fohol to celebrate the victory and the re-emergence of the Prols. Special invitations were sent to all the relations and friends of the Prols on this auspicious occasion. Anga of Angus, Mohan and Rahul of Port Aigcatlos, sons of Arywiel, Siril and her son Liran were the special invitees. Soon all of them arrived for this grand occasion. Trilock was delighted when he beheld his son Liran, who was now a handsome young man with a robust body and fine features. How happy he would be to see his son be a suitable match for the lovely Uttara!

He translated his thoughts into action when he proposed to the king that he should give the hand of his daughter Uttara in marriage to his son Liran. King Viralius was only too glad to refuse this offer. Preparations were soon afoot for the wedding of this young couple. There was great merry making and celebration in the palace as guests and friends poured into the palace for the grand wedding ceremony of this young couple. The marriage was performed with all the rituals and chanting of sacred mantras and the two young hearts were joined for a happy and prosperous married life. Little did they know that their joy would be very short lived as we shall learn shortly.

Peace Emissaries & War Preparations:

ᵀHE ᴬSSEMBLY:

ᴬ fter the end of the celebrations of the marriage of
Uttara and Liran, the Prols along with King
Viralius and their allies huddled in council to plan their
strategy of dealing with the Telhoths. The Prols had
fulfilled all the obligations of their twelve years of exile
and the thirteenth year of concealment successfully
without being detected by any one. Now that that
period was over, it was their right to demand the return
of their kingdom. The Prols had paid heavily for their
folly of playing dice with the cunning Telhoths but now
they had fulfilled their pledge and they wanted to live
in peace and harmony with their cousins. They
therefore conferred among themselves about their
future course of action. Some suggested a reconciliatory
approach to the whole thing while others thought of a
harsh line if the Telhoths refused to cooperate. They
would even be willing to go to war with the Telhoths.

King Anga, the father of Arywiel who had still not
forgotten the humiliations that his daughter had
suffered, wanted to take harsh measures, while Mohan

suggested a milder approach of reconciling with the Telhoths and avoiding a war that would surely bring death and destruction. Many in the assembly supported this view while some thought that this path of peace was futile as the Telhoths were stubborn and were not ready for any conciliation. But Mohan stuck to his position and proposed that negotiations with the Telhoths should be started at once to find a peaceful solution to the problem.

*E*MISSARIES:

A special envoy was sent to the court of the Telhoths. He explained to the Telhoths that the period of exile for the Prols had expired and, since all the conditions of the contract had been fulfilled, the Telhoths should return the half of the kingdom that belonged to the Prols. Assura was furious but Godash calmed him down, saying that the Prols' demand was legitimate and honorable and should be considered favorably. But Karna sided with Assura and even Lohas supported them, saying that the Prols should give up their claim to the throne. Godash did not know what to say, and so it was decided to send an envoy to the Prols asking them to give up their claim to the kingdom or be ready to face war. Soruz was selected to be the emissary of the Telhoths to negotiate with the Prols.

Soruz came to the Fohol where the Prols were staying and told them of the tough stand taken by Assura. He advised them to give up their claim to the kingdom and make peace with the Telhoths. Vilmaril was troubled by the strange demand of Lohas and pleaded with Soruz, "How can we give up our demand of half the kingdom? We are not asking for more. Our demand is just." But Soruz said, "Assura has become mad with pride. He is not ready to reason. He is not ready to listen even to Godash. What can I do?"

When Vilmaril saw that there was no sense in arguing, he reflected for a while and then said, "All right. I am ready to forgo the kingdom for the sake of peace. Let my cousins keep the kingdom. But at least give us five villages, one for each of the brothers. Is this too much I am asking for?" Soruz saw that this was a reasonable demand. But all the other Prols were shocked to hear this and they did not support Vilmaril in asking only for five villages. Vilmaril, however, tried to convince his brothers to agree to this so that a disastrous war could be avoided. Finally, after much persuasion everybody agreed to Vilmaril's view and Soruz left the place with some satisfaction that war could finally be avoided because of the magnanimous offer of the Prols.

Soruz came back to Hastin and narrated his experience at Fohol. He revealed the generous attitude of the Prols and particularly that of Vilmaril. Lohas was pleased with the Prols' request and said that it should be granted without delay. Other elders also agreed with this view, but Assura was adamant. He called the Prols cowards and refused to give them even an iota of land. He was intoxicated with power and was not ready to see reason.

THE MISSION:

After Soruz had left for Hastin, there was much consultation among the Prols and their allies. Everybody agreed that a war should be averted at any cost, so it was decided that a final attempt should be made to make the Telhoths understand the gravity of the situation. For this purpose, Mohan offered himself to serve as an emissary of the Prols and decided to go to Hastin. When Lohas learned about Mohan's visit, he decreed a magnificent welcome for him. Welcoming arches were installed on the roads and special pavilions were erected at every corner of the road. Crowds of people assembled everywhere as they waved and welcomed this special emissary of the Prols.

Mohan was warmly greeted by Lohas, Vidura, Godash, Drona and others. Mohan also consulted Assura and convinced him of the futility of war. He told him that the best course for both the Prols and Telhoths was to live in peace. Assura thought that Mohan was partial to the Prols and did concern himself about the Telhoths. But Mohan told him that the Prols were on the right path of truth and justice and that Assura should offer the hand of friendship to them. Assura was in no mood to compromise and thought that Mohan was favoring the Prols at the cost of the Telhoths.

So he secretly laid a trap to capture Mohan with the help of Amon. "Pounce on him and capture him," he told Amon. Everyone was shocked to hear this. "How can you capture an emissary? It is against all norms of civilized society," people shouted. But Amon rushed forward to tie Mohan up with ropes. Just then a miracle took place. Mohan revealed his divine form and was seen by everyone everywhere in the kingdom. There was pandemonium in the hall. In this uproar and confusion Mohan vanished from their sight and left the palace. Mohan's mission was a failure. A war between the Telhoths and Prols was inevitable. Assura had realized his blunder and after few days apologized to Mohan. Mohan pardoned him after warning him. Their relationship was reconciled.

SEARCH FOR ALLIES:

Mohan came back from Hastin quite dejected that his mission had been a failure. Now there was no escape from the certain war between the Prols and Telhoths. Vilmaril, who had expected that Mohan would bring about peace between the two groups, was also disheartened. He saw no prospect of peace between the two. Mohan decided to return to his capital, Port Aigcatlos. Now that a war was a certainty, both the parties began to search for allies in the war. Mohan had a large and well-trained army so it was natural for both Trilock and Assura to solicit his help in the event of the war.

Assura was the first to reach Port Aigcatlos. He was shown the bed chamber of Mohan. But Mohan was fast asleep and Assura did not wish to disturb him so he sat near the place where Mohan was reclining on a pillow. Just then Trilock also arrived. He, too, saw Mohan sleeping and so quietly sat down at the feet of Mohan. After awhile Mohan woke up and saw Trilock sitting at his feet. He saw Trilock first. Later on he saw Assura sitting by his side. Both of them asked Mohan to help them in the ensuing war. Mohan was puzzled. Both of them were his relatives and he did not wish to displease any one. But Assura cried out, "I have come here first, so you should be on my side." Mohan agreed to this but he said, "I saw Trilock first so I must help him too." There was a quarrel between them. Both claimed Mohan's support in the war.

Then after thinking for a while Mohan said, "Both of you are my kin and I am bound to help both of you. I cannot be partial to any one. So I will leave it to you to decide. I have my armies. You may choose my armies or me. The choice is yours." Since Assura was the first to arrive he was given the chance to choose first. Assura said, "I wish to have your armies." Trilock said, "I am satisfied to have you, Mohan, as my companion in the battle. I wish nothing more." Assura thought he had the better part but Trilock was quite happy in the company of Mohan.

THE TWO WAR CAMPS:

Assura was very happy to have the mighty army of Mohan with him. In addition to this he had the support of Jaralius, Sushol of Trigartas and Shalya of Madra, who, though he was a close relation of Nakula and Shakula, was cunningly tricked into taking sides with Assura. Over and above this, there were Lohas, Godash, Drona, Karna, Kripa, Sakuni, Ashwa and all the other Telhoths. Assura was sure to win the war with such an assemblage of the most powerful warriors along with all the weaponry and huge armies. Assura had eleven divisions of the army against the seven divisions of the Prols.

In the Prol camp there were Vilmaril, Hugo, Trilock, Nakul, Shakula and Mohan. Though Mohan would not take part in the fighting directly, his advice would be most beneficial to the Prols. The Prols appointed King Anga, Drishta, King Viralius, Sikhandi, Tyaki, Chetikana and Hugo as the commanders of the seven divisions of the army. Besides them, there were Liran,

Trilock's son, Fioril, Hugo's son, Prince Kumar, King Viralius's son, and other warriors.

Both the armies lined up on the famous battleground of Goibur ready to enter a terrible war which would cause the deaths of thousands of soldiers from both sides.

THE WAR BEGINS:

Before the actual battle could begin, both the sides formulated codes of conduct for during and after the war. The day's fight would begin in the morning and continue till sunset. There could be friendly contact at night. Single combat should be between equals only. Verbal fight would match verbal fight, horse warrior with horse warrior and chariot fights would be between chariot fighters only. Deserters would not be killed and those who surrendered were to be treated humanely. In the same way those who were not directly involved with the war like the drummers, conch blowers, charioteers, flag bearers and others were to be protected.

The first day of the battle finally dawned and both the armies stationed themselves opposite each other. It was a glorious sight. Flags of various colors fluttered all over the battlefield. Conches blew and the sound of drums filled the air. As the various divisions of the army positioned themselves, Trilock advanced with Mohan driving his chariot. When Trilock moved forward, he saw before him all his elders lined up. There was the grandsire, Godash, who was the oldest and most honored and respected soldier of all. Then there was Drona, the greatest teacher of all, ready with his bow and arrow. Karna, Kripa, and others followed. There was a whole galaxy of warriors who were his kin. When he saw them, Trilock's mind began to waver. "Is it for this day that I have been born and brought up that I may kill my near and dear ones? What is the use of such a war in which brother fights a brother, a disciple kills his own teacher, a young one kills his elder? Then addressing Mohan he asked, "O Mohan, tell me what I should do? I don't know what my duty is. Ultimately what is the purpose of this bloody war? Is it only to secure a few acres of land?"

Mohan was also disturbed by the intense feelings of Trilock for his relations. He too could plainly see the futility of war. But he had more sublime thoughts in his mind. So he enlightened Trilock with these thoughts. He lifted Trilock from the purely mundane to the spiritual and supernatural. Trilock was almost lifted from the earthly or worldly sphere to the heavenly sphere. Mohan then gave his supreme discourse to Trilock, the message of LIFE. He led him from the material to the spiritual. He explained to him the meaning of life and death. He revealed to him the three ways to reach the Almighty, the path of action, the path of knowledge and the path of devotion. Now was the time for Trilock to follow the path of action. He should not worry about what would be the outcome of his actions. He must perform his duty. And as a warrior it was his duty to fight the war, come what may.

Mohan also revealed his divine form to Trilock. Trilock forgot where he was. He was lost in the realm of pure spirit. He was thrilled to see the pure divine form of Mohan. This vision changed the heart of Trilock completely. Then the vision vanished and he was back to his senses with the dull reality of the battlefield. How he would have loved to continue enjoying the heavenly vision for a longer time! But that was not to be.

He now understood the true meaning of life. He was now prepared to fight the war even if it meant the slaying of his own beloved people. He took up arms. He was not bothered about whether his action would bring him glory or ignominy, honor or dishonor.

So the great battle of Goibur began. Vilmaril, the righteous, prostrated before Godash, the most respected of the Telhoth clan, and asked for his blessings. Then he saluted his teacher, Drona, and took his blessings before entering the battle-field. Both of them blessed him, saying that his was the path of righteousness and victory was his. Thus encouraged, Vilmaril jumped into the battle.

Godash began to move around the battlefield with his chariot, destroying everyone who came in his way. Liran, the young son of Trilock, then entered the fray.

Though young, he fought like a veteran warrior, causing destruction among the Telhoths. On the other hand, Salya encountered Kumar, the young son of King Viralius and killed him. This infuriated his brother, Sveta, who charged vehemently at the enemy. But Godash made short work of Sveta. With this the first day of battle ended with the Telhoths proving themselves superior to the Prol forces.

Every day both Prols and Telhoths employed new strategies to win the war. There were duels between Trilock and Godash, Drona and Adumy, Assura and Hugo. Then Liran and Yaki attacked Godash's chariot and almost immobilized it. It was the day for the Prols as they overpowered the Telhoths everywhere.

The following day the Prols again proved superior to the Telhoths. Liran and Yaki attacked the forces of Sakuni and destroyed them while Hugo and his son, Fioril, attacked Assura and demoralized his army. This enraged Godash who charged at the Prols and killed a few thousand men of the Prol army. Stirred up by Mohan, Trilock also came in his full form and with his "Earth-Fire" destroyed thousands of warriors and horses and elephants belonging to the Telhoths.

Godash Is Wounded:

Thus the great war went on day after day. Godash seemed to grow stronger every day. No one could face the great son of Urila. It was said that the only occasion when Godash's strength would fail him was when he would be challenged by a woman or a eunuch. The Prols learned about this, so on the tenth day Trilock put Shikhandi, wearing woman's dress, before his chariot and attacked Godash.

Seeing a woman, Godash's strength failed him. He would not face or challenge a woman. It was below his dignity. Trilock realized that this was his glorious chance to attack Godash. He could not miss this opportunity and he sent a shower of arrows at Godash and pierced him with arrows all over his body. Godash fell from the chariot, but he did not die. Godash finally used the boon 'Death at will' he had been blessed with by his father King Sundry when he had impressed his father by bringing over Yavati and sacrificing his right to be the King. The boon was that he would not die until he himself wished to die.

Thus Godash lay there on the battlefield pierced with arrows all over his body. His body was lifted above the earth and not a part of his body touched the earth. His head was the only place which was not touched by an arrow. As he could not balance his head properly he cried out, "Give me a pillow to rest my head". So they brought him soft, silken pillows to lay his head on. But he would not have any. He desired something else. Trilock understood what Godash wished for. He let go three arrows which pierced the earth and settled just below Godash's head. Now Godash could rest his head on the pillow formed by the arrows. Next, he wished to have water as his mouth was dry. "Give me water," he cried. Again Trilock understood what Godash wanted. He shot an arrow into the earth and there came out a jet of pure water from the underworld, the river Urila. Godash quenched his thirst from the water of his mother, Urila. Godash lay there on the bed of arrows on the battlefield as the war continued. Even at this stage how Godash wished that the war would come to an end! So he summoned Assura and Karna and advised them to end the war and make peace with the Prols. He said that the Prols' was the path of righteousness and truth. They would surely win the war. But neither Assura nor Karna was ready to listen to Godash. So the war continued with renewed vigor.

DRONA AND VILMARIL:

After Godash was wounded, the Telhoth's had to choose a new leader, a new commander-in-chief in place of Godash. Karna was the natural choice. But Karna refused to accept the post and recommended Drona to take that place. Drona was a great teacher and respected by all. He was asked to take up the responsibility of the commander-in-chief. So Drona took charge of the army. It was the eleventh day of the war. Assura advised Drona that he should capture Vilmaril alive so that the rest of the Prols would lose courage and then victory would be theirs. Drona agreed to this suggestion. Changing tactics he attacked Vilmaril and tried to capture him. Just then Trilock arrived and a terrible battle ensued, in which Trilock routed the enemy forces and foiled Drona's plan to capture Vilmaril.

On the twelfth day, Sushol of Trigarta decided to attack with a new strategy of employing a suicide squad and killing Trilock who had created havoc in the Telhoth camp. But this suicide squad was no match for Trilock who wiped out the whole squad by himself.

On the other side, Hugo was attacked by an elephant rider riding on his famous elephant, Supritika. The elephant charged at Hugo and tried to crush him, but Hugo cleverly escaped and hid under the belly of the creature and everyone thought that Hugo was dead. Trilock suddenly appeared on the scene and charged at the elephant rider. Hugo surfaced from under the elephant and killed Supritika.

THE WEB OF SNAKES:

The young warrior Liran, the son of Trilock, was proving to be a menace to the Telhoths. So six mighty Telhoth warriors were engaged to attack Liran. Drona, Ashwa, Kripa, Karna, Brihad and Kritaluz arranged themselves into a snake-like formation and charged at Liran. The boy had to face the enemies from every side. Karna attacked him from behind, which was a very shameful act. Liran's chariot was destroyed by Drona while his bow and arrows were broken by Karna. The boy was defenseless against the six mighty warriors of the Telhoths. Yet he took his sword and shield and jumping out of his chariot began to face the charging enemy. But it was too much for him. Finally, the enemy made short work of him and the boy fell dead on the ground. It was the most shameful strategy that the enemy had used to kill Liran. When Trilock learned of the fate of his son he could not control himself. He knew that it was Kritaluz who was really responsible for the death of his son, and he vowed that the following morning he would slay Kritaluz before sunset and thus avenge the death of his son. If he failed, then he would retire from the battle.

𝕶RITALUZ 𝕴S 𝕾LAIN:

𝕬 ll night on that fateful day there was mourning and sorrowing over the death of Liran. Siril, Liran's mother, was inconsolable while Uttara, the wife of Liran who had now become a widow at a young age, wished to enter the pyre and die along with her husband. But Trilock restrained her saying that she had to live, if not for herself at least for the sake of the unborn child that was in her womb.

It was the fourteenth day of the great war when Trilock would redeem the pledge that he taken the previous night. The Prols prepared themselves for the big battle. Kritaluz was greatly frightened for his life but the other Telhoths gave him courage and Assura promised that no harm would come to him. Then Trilock attacked, piercing his chariot through the Telhoth army. There was panic and confusion among the Telhoths. Drona and Assura came to the rescue of Kritaluz and did not allow Trilock's chariot to reach where Kritaluz was. The fight went on from noon to evening and still Trilock could not succeed in his mission. He wondered whether Kritaluz would escape death and whether his vow would remain unfulfilled. In the meantime Mohan was watching everything. He knew what to do. He covered the evening sun in a cloud of mist. It became dark. Everyone thought that it was evening. But Trilock had not given up hope. He entered the enemy line and went as far as where Kritaluz was hiding. Mohan was guarding everything. Suddenly with his supernatural power he cleared the sky and the golden disc of the sun was seen. Trilock at once pounced on Kritaluz and cut off his head with a powerful arrow. Trilock had kept his promise of killing Kritaluz before the sun set on that day.

In another duel, Karna and Fioril were caught in a terrible fight. In this moment of crisis, Karna forgot what he was doing and in a fit of anger fired the most formidable weapon given him by Lord of Thunder, the Thunderbolt. It struck Fioril on the chest and knocked him down dead. However, soon Karna realized his mistake. He knew that he could use the great weapon given to him by Lord of Thunder only once. Now that it was used up he would be powerless before Trilock.

THE DEATH OF DRONA:

It was now the fifteenth day. With the loss of his son, Fioril, Hugo had almost lost his will to live. Similarly Trilock too was grieving the death of his son though he had vanquished his great enemy, Kritaluz. Both the Prols and the Telhoths had put aside all the codes of conduct and were using ways of treachery and deceit. Drona was as powerful as ever and it was difficult to kill him. Just then Mohan thought of one more trick to kill Drona. Drona had a son whose name was Ashwa. If at any time during the course of the war Drona came to know that his son was killed, he would give up all desire to fight. So Mohan told Trilock to shout loudly, "Ashwa is killed".

Trilock was not willing to employ this mean trick but Hugo had no such scruples. Suddenly charging at an elephant called Ashwa, Hugo cried out loudly, "Ashwa has been killed." When Drona heard this cry, he could not believe it but Hugo cried all the more louder, "Ashwa is dead. Ashwa is dead." Even Vilmaril, the righteous repeated the same, "Ashwa is dead". He had in his mind the elephant Ashwa. Now Drona had no doubt in his mind that his own dear son had been killed. His heart sank with grief. Just then Dhrista rushed there and grasping the grey-white hair of Drona, cut off his head. It was a killing, a very foul killing committed in daylight. It was committed with treachery. Vilmaril cursed himself for the falsehood that he had uttered. Even Trilock and Yaki felt sorry for what had happened. Ashwa, the son of Drona, was the most forlorn as he had lost his dear father by cunning and deceit.

ᴅᴏw Ꞇᴏ Ꞙᴠᴇɴɢᴇ Ꝺʀᴏɴᴀ's Ꝺᴇᴀᴛʜ:

shwa wanted to avenge his father's death. He complained to Vilmaril that though he was called "The Righteous," the king of righteousness, he had used the foulest means to kill his dear father. Vilmaril had no answer. Ashwa was determined to get rid of the murderer of his father. He entered the battlefield with a new vigor. He was armed with the most dangerous weapon of all, the Narayana weapon. He would use that weapon and destroy all the Prols and their army. Even Mohan knew the destructive power of the Narayana weapon. So finally Ashwa fired his only and most powerful weapon. It shot hundreds of missiles into the enemy line. Mohan, who knew the power of this weapon, knew how to escape its effects, so he told the Prols to lay down their arms and lie flat on the ground. The missiles were flying all over the battlefield but they were unable to hurt the enemy. The only one who was foolhardy enough to face the missiles was Hugo. He tried to challenge the missiles but Mohan hastened to the spot and advised Hugo to lay down his arms and lie down on the ground. Hugo finally obeyed Mohan's warning and lay down. The Narayana weapon had no effect. It withdrew itself and came back to Ashwa without harming the enemy.

Ashwa was completely disappointed and left the battlefield. Just then the sage Yasa appeared to him. So Ashwa asked him, "Please tell me why the Narayana weapon had no effect on the enemy." The sage replied, "This weapon has effect only on the enemy that dared to challenge it. It does not have any effect if the enemy submits to it and gives up arms. Mohan knew the secret of this, so he had told his men to surrender before the weapon and they would not be harmed by it. That is what the Prols did and the weapon withdrew itself without doing any harm to them." But sage Yasa said to Ashwa, "There in no need for you to be sad as your father has gone to heaven." This thought brought some consolation to Ashwa and he left the field.

The Prols were happy that the war had gone in their favor while the Telhoths were completely dejected as they had lost their most dear leaders, Godash and Drona.

KARNA - THE COMMANDER

After the death of Drona, the Telhoths appointed Karna as the commander-in-chief of their army. Though the Prols' victory was a foregone conclusion, the Telhoths would not give up. As true warriors they would fight till the finish. Victory or defeat was part of the war. So the war continued with the same vigor as before.

It was the sixteenth day of the war. Hugo and Amon came face to face with each other. Hugo had been waiting for this day. He remembered the way Amon had dragged Arywiel into the court and humiliated her. It was then that he had taken the vow of killing Amon in the most cruel and unmerciful manner. Now his time had come. Hugo rushed at Amon and threw him to the ground. He took the hands and legs of Amon one by one and after having twisted them he broke them. Then in a moment of frenzy he stood on the body of Amon and danced on his body which was soaked with blood. He had kept his promise of killing Amon in the most inhuman way.

118

Elsewhere, Nakula tried to challenge Karna but he was no match for the mighty Karna who almost disarmed Nakula by knocking down his bows, charioteer, sword and mace. But Karna spared Nakula's life, keeping in mind his promise to his mother Noralius that he would not kill her son. Assura and Vilmaril also fought each other violently and Vilmaril would have certainly killed him but he did not, since he wanted Hugo to have that honor. Hugo had not forgotten the taunts of Assura showing his thighs and slapping them while Arywiel was being disrobed.

THE DUEL OF WIZARDS:

Karna was determined to defeat the Prols and kill Trilock. He asked Salya to be his charioteer and lead him to the front. So Salya took his place in the chariot and drove Karna into the battle. Karna and Trilock came face to face. All eyes were on them. It is said that even the gods watched this formidable battle between the two warriors. It was going to be the decisive battle for if Trilock was killed by Karna it would be the end of the war for the Prols. Trilock asked Mohan, "What if I am killed in this duel against Karna!" But Mohan assured him that in case that happened, he would destroy both Karna and Salya. This assurance gave courage to Trilock and he readied himself to face Karna.

At this point Ashwa came to Assura and warned him that Trilock was too powerful for Karna and there was danger to Karna's life. He advised him to call off the war and make peace with the Prols. Assura understood the gravity of the situation but said that it was too late to go back at this stage. They had to fight till the end.

So the duel between Trilock and Karna began. They rushed at each other like two hawks rushing at a prey. They discharged arrows at each other. Then they started using their various weapons. Trilock fired his "Earth-Fire" weapon which was repulsed by Karna. Karna then remembered his favorite weapon, Sakti, which was given to him by Lord of Thunder. But he could not use that weapon as it had already been used on Fioril. So he discharged the serpent weapon at Trilock. He aimed the weapon at the head of Trilock. If successful, it would cut off Trilock's head.

Mohan was quick to fathom the situation. He at once held the reins of the horses and giving a jerk made the horses bend and lower themselves. The chariot too sank a little into the ground. The result was that the serpent weapon could not hurt Trilock's head. It simply knocked the crown from Trilock's head. Karna was disappointed. His heart sank. His only chance to kill Trilock had been foiled. Now he realized that the odds were against him.

Just then the wheel of his chariot got stuck in the ground and could not move. Karna was helpless. He asked Trilock to be considerate. "Please allow me to extricate the chariot wheel," he pleaded. But Trilock would not listen to any such entreaty. Mohan interrupted and taunted Karna, "Where was your justice when Arywiel was being humiliated in the court? Where was your justice when Liran was being attacked by seven warriors at the same time? Wasn't it your duty to persuade Assura to return the kingdom to the Prols at the end of their exile?"

Karna had no answer to these questions of Mohan. Full of shame, he continued fighting against all odds. Trilock's arrows pierced him throughout his body and he was bleeding profusely, but he went on fighting like a true warrior. He was able to wound Trilock on his hand. At this juncture, Mohan ordered Trilock to put an end to this fight by employing the celestial weapon. Trilock remembered the divine weapon that he had obtained from his stay in the Horodus mountains, and he discharged the divine weapon on the enemy.

The arrow went straight at the head of Karna and cut it off. The head fell to the ground and so did the body of Karna. That was the end of this wonderful warrior. News of Karna's death was reported to Assura who was unable to control himself over the loss of his dear friend and commander-in-chief.

Though Trilock had vanquished his foe, he was downcast and unhappy. The Prol victory was now assured and yet Trilock felt unhappy at the means they had used to attain such victory. The Prols were as guilty as the Telhoths in following the path of untruth and falsehood. But the war was not yet over.

THE NEW COMMANDER:

After the death of Karna, the Telhoths were without a commander. Assura conferred with Kripa who suggested that the war should be ended now. The Telhoths had lost all their able commanders and thousands of soldiers. It was no use to stretch the war out any longer. Assura should meet the Prols and reconcile with them so that all of them would be able to live in peace.

Assura, however, was in no mood for reconciliation. He had lost his near and dear ones. He had lost Godash, Drona and Karna who were the most outstanding warriors. He would do them a disservice if he gave up arms at this stage and accepted defeat. It would be an insult to those noble leaders and to all those who had perished in the war. No compromise was possible with the Prols. The only course was that they must continue the war even if it meant losing it. They must fight like gallant soldiers and not like cowards.

So on the eighteenth day Assura approached Salya and begged him to take up the challenge of leading the Telhoth army in battle against the Prols. Salya accepted the challenge and vowed to kill Mohan and Trilock and thus avenge the death of Karna. So Salya became the commander-in-chief of the Telhoth army.

The Prols knew that Salya was no ordinary soldier. He was a brave fighter and it would not be easy to vanquish him. So the battle started between the two armies on the eighteenth day. As most of the solders had been killed in the last fifteen days, the armies of both sides were considerably diminished. Vilmaril stood up to counter Salya's might. In this he was helped by his brother Hugo, who immobilized Salya's chariot. Then, like a wounded lion, Salya charged at the Prols and began to slaughter them. The Telhoths saw a new hope. Vilmaril came face to face with Salya. He took up his spear and attacked Salya, piercing him with the weapon. Salya could not resist and fell down dead.

In another encounter, Nakula challenged Sakuni, the master gambler and uncle of Assura, and killed his son. This infuriated Sakuni who charged at Nakula but Shakula came to his rescue and made short work of Sakuni. Thus he exterminated the man who was the real cause of the war between the Prols and the Telhoths. Sakuni was the one who had advised Assura to play a game of dice which ultimately led the two parties to the bitterest of all wars.

ᴅEATH ᴏF ᴀSSURA:

f the mighty Telhoths, Assura was the last one. As he looked at the deserted and desolate vast plains of Goibur, Assura had mixed feelings. He felt sorry for the plight of the Telhoths. He realized that it was due to him that this unnecessary war was fought. Had he made peace with the Prols, both the cousins would have lived in peace and he could have avoided this great tragedy of losing his loved ones. He had nowhere to hide. Shortly he came to a lake known as Dwai Lake. Assura entered the cool waters of the lake. The cool waters gave him some comfort as he lay there hiding among the weeds.

The Prols wondered where Assura had vanished. They started to look for him everywhere. They did not want him to escape so they sought him everywhere. They finally found him in the lake. "Come out of the lake, Assura, and fight with us. Why are you hiding yourself here in the lake like a coward?" they shouted. Assura could not bear these taunts. He said, "What am I to do now? All my dear brothers are dead. I am not interested in the kingdom any more. Go and take my kingdom and rule over it." But Vilmaril was quick to reply, "It was all your doing, Assura. What is the use of complaining now? You were the cause of all the trouble. Had you acted wisely upon the advice of your elders, you would not have seen this day. But now you must come out and fight. We do not wish to have the gift of your kingdom from you." "But I am without arms. How am I to fight five of you single-handed?" Assura asked. To this Vilmaril replied, "Don't worry. We will supply you with weapons. And you will fight with us one at a time."

Assura had no other option but to fight. So he came out of the weeds in the lake. The Prols told him to choose any weapon that he desired. He chose a mace for his weapon and decided to fight with Hugo. It was a terrible duel of maces between the two. Assura was no ordinary soldier. He was an adept fighter with his mace. For a time it seemed that Hugo was losing the battle. Just then Mohan made a sign to Hugo, showing him his thigh. Hugo remembered the day when Assura had repeatedly shown his thigh in front of Arywiel and challenged the Prols. Now Hugo's anger surged forth with hatred for the man who had insulted him and lifting his mighty mace he attacked Assura and struck him with the mace on his thigh and broke it. Assura was crippled and fell down on the ground. As he lay there he reprimanded Hugo for hitting him below the belt. It was not befitting a true warrior. But Hugo had no qualms of conscience. Assura had deserved what he got. The Prols left Assura and departed from there, leaving Assura writhing in pain and waiting for his death.

Then there came to him others of his loyal friends and gave him company till his last moments.

𝕿HE 𝕰VIL 𝕬CT:

𝕷ooking at Assura, Ashwa was filled with rage and in a fit of anger he vowed that he would kill the Prols that night and thus avenge the death of his father and also the deaths of Godash and Karna and all the other Telhoths. "I will avenge you, O Assura! I will kill every one of the Prols." Assura was pleased with Ashwa and appointed him the solitary commander of the Telhoth army.

In the dark of the night Ashwa along with his companions, slipped into the Prol camp and brutally butchered Dhristas, the five sons of Arywiel who were fast asleep in the camp. Only Mohan, Yaki and the five Prols escaped death as they were in another camp. When Assura heard of this, he found some solace in it and peacefully he breathed his last. Ashwa, however, escaped from the scene and was never discovered by anyone.

Hearing the news of the death of her five sons, Arywiel was inconsolable and vowed that she would not rest till the murderer, Ashwa, was killed by the Prols. But the Prols could not locate Ashwa anywhere. Hugo, along with Mohan and Trilock, continued their search for Ashwa and finally spotted him hiding behind sage Yasa on the bank of the river Urila. A terrible fight arose between him and the Prols. Ashwa then discharged the most formidable weapon of all, the Brahma weapon. Mohan advised Trilock to use his divine weapon to counteract the Brahma weapon. Then again at the advice of Mohan, Trilock cleverly withdrew the weapon, but Ashwa did not know how to withdraw his weapon so it flew towards the womb of Uttara. Fortunately, Mohan who was aware of this, intervened and came to the rescue of the unborn child. He with his supernatural powers deflected the weapon towards Ashwa himself, hitting him and killing him instantly. Thus Liran's son was saved from destruction. Hearing of this development Arywiel became pacified.

The End Of The War:

The great war of Goibur finally came to an end after eighteen days. It was a war of death and destruction. The Telhoths had lost their greatest leaders including Drona, Karna, and Assura while Godash lay waiting for his end to come. News of the war reached the blind king Lohas daily as he was told every day of the day's happenings. As he heard of the death of his dear sons, Lohas grieved and cried. He could not bear the thought that the Telhoths were losing the battle on every side. On the final day, when he heard that the Telhoths had lost the war and practically all his children had perished in the war, Lohas could bear it no longer. He began to moan and weep.

The Prols slowly made their way to Hastin to their uncle Lohas. Vilmaril was not a happy man as he went up to his uncle to embrace him. Broken in spirit and still crying, Lohas embraced Vilmaril and shed many a tear. He did not scold Vilmaril or become angry with him as he realized that Vilmaril was not the only one responsible. He himself was equally responsible for the great calamity. In fact, Vilmaril had tried every means to avoid the war but it was all in vain. Lohas blamed himself for not being able to restrain his wayward son, Assura, who was the immediate cause of the war.

Then came Hugo. Lohas smiled and called out to Hugo. "Come, Hugo, Come. Let me embrace you." But Mohan who saw the angry face of Lohas understood at once what he had in his mind. He wanted to crush Hugo to death to avenge the loss of his sons. So in a swift movement Mohan pushed Hugo aside and placed before the blind king the life-size iron image of Hugo. Lohas embraced the iron figure and crushed it into many pieces. Hugo was saved by the clever trick of Mohan.

Then the brothers went up to Wardoria, the blindfolded queen mother of Assura, who was weeping profusely and was unconsolable. All the five Prols knelt before her and asked forgiveness of her. She was very magnanimous in forgiving all of them for what they had done. It was sheer destiny and no one could escape it. But, for Mohan, Wardoria had some harsh words since Mohan knew beforehand what was to happen and yet he did not try to prevent the holocaust. "My Lord, you know all things. Why did you not try to act?" she complained. But Mohan knew better. It is not god but man who makes his own destiny. Even gods cannot intervene in this matter. Man can, by his own will and actions make or mar his fate. But Mohan knew that this was beyond the comprehension of the woman.

THE SECRET REVEALED:

oon the king and the queen, along with the Prols, descended the steps of the palace and went down to the banks of the river Urila. There assembled all the people, the mourners, widows, orphaned children and wounded soldiers. They began to chant and pray for the dead. Noralius came forward and embracing Vilmaril closely, she revealed to him the secret that she had kept in her heart. Now she told him that Karna was her own son, born of the sun-god and that he was the elder brother of the Prols. When Vilmaril and the others came to know this, they were surprised. "Why did you not reveal it to us for so many years?" they asked. But she replied in anguish, "Because Karna was indebted to Assura for what he had done in the court to save his honor and wanted to serve him till the end." The Prols forgot all their enmity with their brother, Karna, and paid homage to him, offering prayers and asking for forgiveness for what they had done to him out of ignorance. Similarly cremation ceremonies were performed for all the departed souls. Then they bathed in the sacred river and departed. For almost a month various other ceremonies and obsequies continued for the dead. After all the rituals had been concluded and the Prols had cleansed themselves of all the sins of the past, the question of ascending to the throne and ruling the kingdom arose. Someone had to take up the reins of the state.

ĐEATH ÖF ÖODASH:

𝕿he most obvious choice for the post of the king was naturally Vilmaril. He had already been the emperor of Roshuk and had even performed the Victory ceremony. But Vilmaril's mind was confused. He thought of all the unfortunate things that had happened over so many years and especially during the last eighteen days. The more he thought about it the more he was convinced that becoming a king and ruling the country was not to his liking. He would prefer to retire and go to the forest and lead a life of penance and self-purification. Mohan who had persuaded Trilock to fight the war, though he had shown aversion to the war, again came to the rescue of Vilmaril and made him understand that he had to take charge of the kingdom whether he liked it or not. Even Narad, sage Yasa and other sages came down and explained to Vilmaril that war was inevitable and performing one's duty was of paramount importance.

Vilmaril was finally convinced that he had to take up the mantle of the kingdom. "But I know so little of statecraft and the ways of the world," he objected. To this Mohan replied, "There is one who is thoroughly conversant with all this. He will guide you in everything. You need not worry on that score." Mohan reassured Vilmaril. He had in mind Godash who was still alive and lying on the bed of arrows on the river bank. With this assurance Vilmaril was prepared to take up the heavy responsibility of kingship.

Godash was still alive and was waiting for the course of the sun to breathe his last. There was still time for that. Death would not overtake him as he had the boon of death when he himself wished. So Mohan led Vilmaril to the place where Godash lay on the bed of arrows. When he saw him, Vilmaril was overcome with emotion. Here was the greatest of the Telhoth clan, a giant of a man. He was the greatest fighter of all and at the same time he was equally well-versed in the art of governance. Mohan introduced Vilmaril as the future king and begged Godash to enlighten him in state craft.

Though Vilmaril was his enemy in the war, Godash did not bear any ill-will to him and was ready to help him out. Godash, who had a wealth of knowledge and experience, spoke kindly to Vilmaril. He said,

"My child, it was not your fault that you entered the war. War was thrust upon you and you could not escape it." Vilmaril then replied, "I am completely sick of the war. I do not wish to ascend the throne, which is blood-stained. Instead I would prefer to go to the forest and lead the life of an ascetic and do penance for all the wicked things I have done."

But Godash comforted him saying, "It was not your fault. You did not bring about the war. It was Assura who brought about the war. It is the duty of the warrior to fight. You have done your duty. You have rid the kingdom of the wicked. Though I had fought with the wicked, I had no other motive."

Mohan then requested Godash to throw some light on the duty of the ruler and how to discharge these duties. Godash willingly explained everything in detail to Vilmaril. He knew that Vilmaril, the righteous, would be an ideal king as he had all the qualities of a benevolent king. Daily Vilmaril would come to Godash and Godash in turn would expound the intricacies of statecraft, the qualities of a good king, the management of his subordinates, care of his subjects, relations with the neighbors, treatment of his enemies and all other things related to the duty of a king. A king must not only be virtuous, righteous and merciful, but he should also be firm, bold and just. He should neither be too soft nor too strict. He must be self-controlled and humble. He should be tolerant, but not at the expense of discipline. He should be industrious, diligent and exemplary. Last but not least a King should have love for his subjects for love is the greatest of all virtues.

Throughout all this period of waiting Godash had attained a perfect mastery over body consciousness. Even in this state of trance he had maintained a perfect balance of mind and body. After delivering his message to Vilmaril he was lost in meditation. By now the sun had moved northward and it was the last day of the winter solstice. Godash's wish was fulfilled. He could see the radiance of the sun in all its glory. He prayed to Mohan to allow him to relinquish his body and ascend to the heavens. Mohan blessed him and Godash's soul left for his heavenly abode.

This was the most glorious moment for all who watched him depart from this world. The son of the Urila had finally fulfilled his mission on earth. The last rites were performed and the body of Godash was consigned to the flames. It is said that Urila the goddess came personally to collect the ashes of her son. She was now proud of her son whom she restored to his original state in heaven. All other Arol's who had been cursed by the sage to be born as mortals on earth were already liberated by the Goddess Urila when she drowned them one by one and were in heaven. Godash was the last Arol left on the earth to be rescued as he had completed his mission on earth.

THE GRAND CEREMONY:

Though Vilmaril had taken upon himself the mantle of the king, the carnage that he had witnessed on the battle-field of Goibur still continued to haunt him. Now that he was installed as the king, Mohan and sage Yasa convinced him that he had to perform his duty leaving aside all thoughts of the war. Sage Yasa suggested that the "Peace ceremony" would be very beneficial for this purpose.The peace ceremony was finally performed. Kings and sages attended the ceremony with great enthusiasm and all were immensely pleased to find that Vilmaril's ceremony was second to none.

The ceremony finally came to an end and all the kings and nobles who were invited left the place and went to their respective kingdoms. Mohan also thought that his mission was now complete and that he should return to Port Aigcatlos. So he left for his kingdom.

THE RETURN TO HEAVEN:

hen the war had concluded, Wardoria, the wife of Lohas, had warned Mohan that since he had not done his best to avert the war he too would face the same fate as others and his kingdom would be punished for his pride and arrogance. Once it happened that some sages came to Port Aigcatlos. The citizens received them with reverence but they wanted to test the sages for their wisdom and holiness, so they brought before them a certain young man, dressed up as a woman, and asked them if that woman would bear a son or a daughter. The sages were furious and felt insulted for such a kind of test and cursed them. They said "He would bring forth an iron bar which will be responsible for the destruction of their race," said the sages.

What the sages said came true for the young man called Samva indeed brought forth an iron rod. Being frightened, the young man rushed to Mohan and Rahul, the step brother of Mohan, and asked for their help. Rahul advised him to crush the rod into powder and throw it into the sea. Unfortunately, one small bit of the rod, which no one noticed, remained on the sea shore. Only Mohan knew that this would cause great destruction.

After ruling the kingdom for nearly thirty six years Mohan thought that his earthly existence had now come to an end and that he must retire from this world.

In the meantime the ministers of Port Aigcatlos became more and more proud and resorted to all sorts of vices. The bits of iron left on the sea shore suddenly sprang up into reeds which could be used as weapons. Once, when the ministers had gone for a picnic, they started a quarrel among themselves which developed into a fight. The angry ministers uprooted the weeds and started throwing them at one another. The weeds turned into a powerful weapon and destroyed all of them. That was the end of the Yadava race of Mohan.

After Rahul, having cast off his physical body, had left for heaven, Mohan too went to the forest. As he sat in a yogic posture lost in meditation; he looked like a deer taking rest. It was said that Mohan could not be wounded except in the sole of his foot. When he sat in meditation looking like a deer, a hunter took him for a deer and shot an arrow that hit him in his sole. Mohan turned into his divine form and vanished. Trilock reached Port Aigcatlos and wanted to meet Mohan but he was sorry to hear that Mohan had already left for his heavenly abode.

Trilock was now alone. He invoked sage Yasa and narrated the sad story of all who had left the world. Sage Yasa told him that his mission on this earth had come to an end and so now was his turn to leave the world.

THE PROLS SET OUT FOR HEAVEN:

The five Prols came to know that their earthly existence had now come to an end and they had to leave for the other world. Vilmaril ruled the kingdom for few more years after the war. They appointed Parikul, the son of Liran, as the king of Hastin and Roshuk.

The five Prols along with Arywiel now prepared themselves to go to their heavenly abode. They all walked the land, dressed as ascetics. Arywiel was the last one and they were followed by their favorite dog. They began touring the whole country, beginning with the east. When they came to the sea, Trilock surrendered all his weapons to Varuna, the sea god. They moved south and then northward till they reached the Horodus Mountains. Walking through mountains and valleys they finally came to the mountain peak, Meru, which was the highest point among the Horodus. Arywiel at this point suddenly fell down and died.

In the same way Shakula and Nakula died one after the other. Trilock came next. Hugo wanted to know the reason for Arywiel's death. Vilmaril replied that it was because she was partial to Trilock. "What was the cause of the death of Shakula?" Hugo queried. Vilmaril replied, "Shakula had thought himself superior to the others. That was the cause of his death." Nakula was the next to go because he thought very highly of his own physical beauty. In the same way Trilock died because he was very proud and conceited and thought that he was the sole destroyer of his enemies.

Hardly had Hugo heard the answers to his questions when he fell down. Hugo wondered what crime he had committed. Vilmaril said that it was due to the boastfulness of his physical strength. The only survivor was now Vilmaril and his favorite dog.

Indra, the god of heaven, came down to receive Vilmaril who was angry that his four brothers and Arywiel had fallen and died. Indra then informed him that all his brothers and Arywiel who died were already taken into heaven. "We want you to come to your heavenly abode with your mortal body since you are an exceptional case," Indra told Vilmaril.

"But you must leave this unholy creature that follows you. It cannot be allowed to enter heaven," Indra said to Vilmaril.

Vilmaril then replied, "For me all creatures are equally important. This dog has kept company with us for a long time and has become part of the family. I cannot desert it now."

"If you want to enter heaven and enjoy the company of your brothers and wife, you have to reject this creature," Indra told Vilmaril firmly.

Vilmaril them solemnly replied, "It is my duty to protect the weak and the humble. This dog is my dependent. I shall never desert it. I shall rather forgo the happiness of heaven than give up this dog."

At this point the dog transformed into a radiant god. He pronounced solemnly, "I am proud of you, my son. I still remember the occasion when in the lake you did not show any partiality between your brother and step brother. You had chosen Nakula first instead of the other brothers. Now I wanted to test your compassion for low creatures. I am deeply pleased with your impartiality for the dog and other low creatures. Indra has come to take you to heaven. Please accompany him to heaven and occupy your rightful place there."

Vilmaril then sat in the chariot and he left for the high heavens along with Indra. Others had gone before him but they had cast aside their mortal bodies before entering heaven. Here was a special case of a mortal who entered the heaven with his mortal body. Vilmaril was welcomed by all the gods and heavenly spirits.

THE PROLS IN HEAVEN:

When Vilmaril reached heaven, he had a surprise. He saw that Assura had arrived there before him. He failed to understand how Assura, the most wicked of the Telhoths, had managed to enter heaven so easily. If there was anyone who had committed crimes of the most depraved nature it was Assura. He was greedy, conceited, cunning, haughty, mean and revengeful. In spite of these vices and sins, Assura had entered heaven. Then what was the difference between Assura and the righteous, virtuous and pious himself, who was the symbol of all that was good? Now in heaven both of them seemed to be on par. Both were treated equally. Vilmaril was puzzled.

Narad understood this natural reaction of Vilmaril and explained to him that heaven is not only meant for the pious, holy and righteous. It is also meant for the valiant, brave and daring. Assura had exhibited exceptional bravery in the war and had fought like a true warrior. Hence he deserved to be in heaven as much as the other Prols did. Vilmaril was pacified and reconciled.

Now the first thing that Vilmaril wanted to do in heaven was to look for the Prol brothers and to meet them. Vilmaril was led to the various places of heaven and searched everywhere. He was then led to the gloomiest place which was covered with thorns and thistles, rough roads and was dark and filthy. He heard pitiful sounds of groaning and agony but could not make out where the sounds were coming from. So he enquired from the messenger who accompanied him who they were and why they were groaning so piteously.

The messenger informed him that they were the sounds of none other than his own brothers, and relations, like Godash, Karna, Hugo, Trilock, Nakula, Shakula, and Arywiel. At this Vilmaril wondered how all these righteous men were put in a place that was as bad as hell.

"In that case I do not wish to go to heaven and stay with people like Assura. I would prefer to live here in hell in the company of my dear brothers," said Vilmaril.

At this, there appeared before him Indra and Yama, the god of death. The ugly vision of hell disappeared from before him. The two gods told him that the vision of hell was only a temporary illusion that had been created to test him once more. He had to pass through this stage to wash away any small sins and imperfections he may have. Now that he had gone through that stage, he would be taken to heaven where all his brothers were enjoying the heavenly bliss. Vilmaril was righteous during his life on earth and he had been proved equally righteous here in heaven. So he was escorted to his dear brothers and placed in heaven where he would enjoy the vision of the pure divinity for all time to come.

The End

What is life as told by Mohan.

Life is a Challenge............................Meet it
Life is a Gift................................Accept it
Life is an Adventure............................Dare it
Life is a Sorrow............................Overcome it
Life is a tragedy............................Face it
Life is a Duty..............................Perform it
Life is a Game............................Play it
Life is a Mystery............................Unfold it
Life is a Song...........................Sing it
Life is an Opportunity..............................Take it
Life is a Journey..............................Complete it
Life is a Promise..............................Fulfill it
Life is a Love............................Enjoy it
Life is a Beauty............................Praise it
Life is a Spirit..............................Realize it
Life is a Struggle............................Fight it
Life is a Puzzle....................Solve it
Life is a Goal............................achieve it

LOVE THE TRUTH, BE TRUE TO LOVE

Main Characters And Places For Reference

Amon: Second son of blind King Lohas and Wardoria. Younger brother of cruel Assura. Blind follower of Assura.Very cruel himself. Wants to destroy Prol brothers.

King Anga of Angus: Father of Arywiel and father-in-law of five Prols. Childhood friend of the archery teacher Drona.

Angus: The Kingdom of King Anga. Trilock wins Arywiel here in archery competition.

Arols: The demi god eight brothers living in heaven. Cursed by a sage to be born on earth as mortals. Godash is the eighth brother.

Aruvious: Lohas the blind king (father of the Telhoth brothers) was married to the princess of this kingdom. It was ruled by King Zarus.

Arywiel: Beautiful princes of Angus. Daughter of King Anga.Wife of five Prol brothers.

Ashwa: Son of archery teacher of Hastin, Drona. Mighty warrior himself.

Assura: Ambitious and cruel eldest brother of one hundred Telhoth brothers. Son of Lohas and Wardoria. Aspires to be the king of Hastin.He is jealous of Prols.

Banajara Forest: Prols hide here during their thirteen years in exile.Dense forest with wild animals where only few could survive.

Deolana: Sister of demon Hidimba and wife of Hugo. Has a son through Hugo called Fioril.

Drona: The archery teacher of Kingdom of Hastin. Teaches both Telhoth and Prol brothers.

Fioril: Son of Hugo and Deolana. Helps Hugo in the grand battle of Goibur.

Fohol: Prols spend the thirteenth year in exile here in disguise.

Godash: Son of King Sudry and the river goddess Urila. He takes vow of celibacy. He is one of the Arol brothers from heaven who has been cursed to be born on earth as a mortal. He sacrifices the throne of Hastin for his father's sake. Protector of Hastin. Caretaker of Prols and Telhoths.

Hastin: Capital city of the Lunar kingdom. King Sudry ruled this kingdom. Prols and Telhoths both want to rule this kingdom.

Hidimba: The demon and brother of Deolana.

Horodus mountains: Trilock explores this area to seek divine weapon. He eventually goes below the surface of the Earth to acquire it.

Hugo: The second of Prol brothers. Brave and Strong.

Karna: Secret son of Noralius and the Sun-God out of wedlock when Noralius was only fifteen. His birth was embarrassing to Noralius so she quietly slipped him downstream into a basket into a river. The boat was found by a charioteer. Karna's status as a son of a charioteer (and not of warrior class) leads Prols, particularly Hugo, to spurn his challenge to Trilock at the archery competition, though he is extremely skilled archer. He allies himself to Assura and hopes to kill Trilock in combat, perhaps in a battle. Karna himself and Prols are unaware till the very end that karna is in fact their step brother.

Liran: Brave son of Trilock and Siril. Dies at a young age when he gets caught up in "Web of Snakes" during battle of Goibur.

Lohas: Became King of Hastin after replacing Prol.Father of Assura the eldest of the hundred cruel Telhoth brothers. He was born blind, Lohas lives through the deaths of his sons and the dreadful carnage of the war. His tragedy is he had the power and the authority to prevent the disasters that befell his Kingdom, but he lacked the will to act.

Madri: Second wife of Prol. Mother of Nakula & Shakula. Stepmother of Trilock, Hugo and Vilmaril.

Mohan: The incarnation of God.The main character of the great epic. Philosophical and Spiritual guide to Kingdom of Hastin.

Mt.Apex: Hugo (strongest of Prol brothers) kills the wicked giant Baka here after a ten day fight.

Nakula: The fourth son of Prol and his second wife Madri. Step brother of Vilmaril, Trilock and Hugo.

Noralius: First wife of Prol. Mother of Vilmaril, Trilock and Hugo. Step mother of Nakula and Shakula. She has also a secret son called Karna out of wedlock.

Parikul: The son of Liran becomes the king of Hastin and Roshuk after Prols depart to heaven.

Prol: The pale king, younger brother of the blind Lohas. Father of five wise Prol brothers. Retires as a King after failing health passing on the throne to his blind elder brother Lohas.

Prol brothers: The five wise and brave sons of Prol and Noralius. Bitter rivals of Telhoth brothers who want to snatch away the throne of Hastin and Roshuk from them. The five brothers love each other dearly.

Rahul: Elder brother of Mohan, the god.

Sakuni: Cruel uncle of Assura, the cruel eldest brother of Telhoths. Ace dice player and a gambler. Always helps Assura get rid of Prols.

Shakula: The twin brother of Nakula.The fifth son of Prol and his second wife Madri. Step brother of Vilmaril, Trilock and Hugo.

Sikhandi: He is neither a male nor female.He Kills Godash.

Solmin: The Prols survive the house of wax conspiracy here.

King Sudry: The King of Hastin. Great grandfather of Prols and Telhoths. His blunder causes the divide in the family and ultimately results in the Battle of Goibur.

Telhoth brothers: The hundred cruel sons of King Lohas and Wardoria. The Telhoths are bitter rivals of the Prols. Assura the eldest, is jealous of his cousins the Prols, because they are looked upon as heroes by the people in the Kingdom. Incited by his second brother, Amon, Assura constantly tries to kill, harass, and deceive, the Prols. Assura wants the Kingdom of Hastin and Roshuk for himself.

Trilock: The third of the Prol brothers. Worlds best archer.

River Urila: Primary river in the Indus valley. River goddess Urila resides here when she is not in Heaven.

Vidura: The wise younger brother of Lohas and Prol. Fathered by sage Yasa on a maid girl.

Vilmaril: Eldest of five Prol brothers. Wise, kind hearted, brave and a just ruler.

King Viralius of Fohol: Prols hide in his kingdom during their last year in exile.

Wardoria: The daughter of King Zarus of Aruvious. She marries Lohas. Upon finding out that her husband-to-be was blind, she swore never to enjoy what he could not and blindfolded herself. For the rest of her life, she wore the blindfold. Mother of Assura and other hundres Telhoth brothers.

Sage Yasa: Wise uncle of Prol and Lohas. Advisor to the kingdom of Hastin.

The Writers:

P.Ashar is the CEO of **The SmileySun Media LLC, the creator of this book.** His hobbies are reading, listening to music, and visiting the countryside. He lives with his wife and parents only a few miles away from Princeton University, New Jersey, USA. He does do a few illustrations as a hobby.

Thomas.J.P is a retired school teacher who taught English. He also taught courtesy and humility to his students. He always strived to see that his students became good citizens. He was always loved and respected by his students. He writes during his spare time. P. Ashar is his ex-student.

The Artists:

Jeff Crosby was born and raised in Texas. He came to New York City to attend the MFA Illustration Program at the School of Visual Arts. For nine years he has been freelancing, doing work for both editorial and children's book publishers. He has five children's books published with Grosset & Dunlap including *Coat of*

159

Arms and Dragons. His most recent book is ***Brave Cloelia***, published by Getty Publications. Jeff's work has been selected for inclusion in several illustration annuals such as the Society of Illustrators, Communication Arts, and American Illustration. He currently lives in Manhattan with his wife.

Thomas McAteer is a graduate of West Chester University and studied multimedia design at University of the Arts in Philadelphia. He has traveled across the globe to gather inspiration for his artistic style, painting in Florence, Venice, Budapest, Paris, Vienna, Amsterdam and more. He is the illustrator behind numerous picture books including ***Beakie the Amazonian Wonderdog and The Little White Squirrel's Secret***. He currently resides in the City of Brotherly Love with his family.

Lightning Source UK Ltd.
Milton Keynes UK
07 November 2009

145964UK00001B/16/A